CHAMBER OF DEATH

The window was only a few feet to her left, and in a moment Corson had made up her mind and clambered over the sill. If she was going to die anyway, maybe she could at least kill Lord Thierran first.

But Lady Nyctasia was alone. There was blood on her mouth, and her shirt was torn at the shoulder. She gave no sign of seeing Corson, though her eyes were open and staring.

Corson hurried past her, and flattened herself against the wall by the doorway. Lord Thierran was coming up the corridor, still shouting orders to his retainers. "I want guards at every entrance! Search the stables and the gatehouse!"

He strode across the room to the window and looked out anxiously over the grounds, watching for any movement.

Corson kicked the door shut. At the sound, Lord Thierran wheeled around and stared at her in disbelief. She was coming towards him, smiling, a dagger in her left hand . . .

"I didn't plan to read SILVERGLASS all in one night—I had to, because it's such fun and so darned good!"
—Andrew Offutt

"Filled with colorful characters, fast-paced excitement and plenty of bed-hopping. J.F. Rivkin is a writer to watch!"
—Phyllis Ann Karr
Author of the *Frostflower* books

Ace Books by J. F. Rivkin

SILVERGLASS
WEB OF WIND
WITCH OF RHOSTSHYL
(coming in June)

J.F. RIVKIN
SILVERGLASS

ACE BOOKS, NEW YORK

This book is an Ace original edition, and has never been
previously published.

SILVERGLASS

An Ace Book / published by arrangement with
the author

PRINTING HISTORY
Ace edition / September 1986

ISBN: 0-441-76600-5

Ace Books are published by The Berkley Publishing Group,
200 Madison Avenue, New York, New York 10016.
The name "ACE" and the "A" logo are trademarks belonging to
Charter Communications, Inc.
PRINTED IN THE UNITED STATES OF AMERICA

10 9 8 7 6 5 4 3

Acknowledgments

The author would like to extend thanks to the following persons for their very generous help and encouragement: Piers Anthony, Phyllis Ann Karr, Fritz Leiber, Richard K. Lyon, Andrew Offutt, Jessica Amanda Salmonson, and especially Susan Shwartz.

1

THOUGH CORSON BRENN Torisk had not often been to Rhost-shyl, she remembered just where The Lame Fox Tavern was. For some things she had an infallible memory. The Lame Fox was a disreputable den shunned by the respectable people of the city. There was a place like it in every town on the coast, and Corson was familiar with them all.

The crowded alehouse was all one room, filled with tres-tle-tables and benches. The only light came from smoky torches and the great hearth where joints of meat roasted and charred. On every side men and women were drinking and dicing, arguing loudly, cursing and bragging. A singer with a small lap-harp was perched on a table, trying to make herself heard above the din.

The crowd eyed Corson curiously as she entered, but she was accustomed to that. Her height alone usually drew stares, since people so tall were rare in the north—but no one had ever found her ungainly. She moved with an athlete's grace and power, and her beauty was not hidden by her travel-worn tunic and breeches. She had large blue eyes, and skin of a warm, rich gold. After her release from the army, she had let her chestnut hair grow long as a mark of her independence. She usually kept it plaited in a braid and bound like a crown around her brow, but when she let it down, it fell over her broad shoulders and straight, tapered back in a rippling tawny wave.

Corson's only ornament was a pair of small golden ear-rings—the trophy of an early exploit. She'd been hired by a merchant guild to rid the roads of a certain dangerous bandit. The earrings had been his.

She met all stares at The Lame Fox with a look of deliberate challenge that made the curious drop their eyes hastily, or turn away. Her confident manner declared that she was well able to use the battered broadsword that hung at her hip. She took a seat near the singer and ordered a tankard of the best ale. Everyone knew that the ale all came from the same barrel, but the more you paid the less water they added to your portion.

Corson was feeling very well pleased with herself. She had just been hired by both the leading families of Rhostshyl to assassinate the same person. And neither party knew of her dealings with the other. The rival houses of Edonaris and Teiryn had been lethal political enemies for generations, and the city was on the brink of civil war. It seemed they could only agree on this one thing—both were willing to pay a high price for the death of the sorceress, Lady Nyctasia ar'n Edonaris. The Teiryns accused her of causing a fatal sickness among them, and even her own kin were afraid of her. Corson found the situation amusing as well as profitable, and she meant to celebrate her stroke of good fortune by getting prodigiously drunk.

The girl with the harp was singing:

> "Oh, I could complain
> that my life is a curse—
> The wind and the rain
> and the hole in my purse!
> But what would I gain?
> Things could always be worse!"

Corson laughed and tossed a coin to the singer, who caught it in her hand and winked.

Seeing that Corson had money, every gambler, pickpocket and charlatan in the tavern took a renewed interest in her, and she was at once invited to join in a game of death's head.

Corson loved to gamble, but she'd learned from bitter experience that it was fool's sport. "No thanks, I've no luck with dice."

"But tonight your luck may change."

"Ah, but why trust to luck when you can learn fortune's secrets?" A slender young man dressed in bright motley leaned toward her across the table. Around his neck hung a string of medallions stamped with mysterious symbols.

"As well toss your money in the gutter as give it to fortunetellers," sneered the gambler, who felt that she had established her right to swindle Corson first.

Though she had no faith in soothsayers, Corson wanted some amusement and paid the youth what he asked. With a grand gesture, he pushed aside the pitcher and mugs, and drew an eight-pointed star on the table with a stump of charcoal. From a leather pouch he took a handful of polished gemstones and handed them to Corson.

"Will you first hear of the present?" he inquired. At Corson's nod, he drew a circle around the star. "The mirror," he explained, "that shows things as they are. Shake the stones in your hand and throw them on the star. Their pattern will tell the tale."

When Corson had done so, he studied the scattered stones intently, murmuring to himself, "Green at three!" and, "Just on the line, there."

"You are placed at a perilous juncture," he said at last. "The whole course of your fate depends on a choice you will soon make. If you choose ill. . . ." He shook his head solemnly. "No fortune awaits you at all."

"That's an old story," said Corson. "And what if I choose well?"

"To answer that, I must consider the future—thus!" He gathered up the colored stones, then drew a square around the circle. "The window," he proclaimed, "that shows things far off."

Corson threw the stones again, and the fortuneteller contemplated their pattern with evident satisfaction. "Should you choose this way, a dangerous journey lies before you, but at its end fortune will favor you. You will win wealth and honors and become a lady of title and influence."

"Oh yes, very likely," laughed Corson. "And what is this fateful choice I must make?"

"You will know it when the time comes. If you wish for surer knowledge now, I can only try—but such secrets are not so easily come by. . ." He paused expectantly. A further payment from Corson would no doubt have eased the difficulty, but at that moment they were interrupted by a shout of indignation from the singer. One of the customers had accused her of picking his pocket.

"I wouldn't go near enough to you to steal your purse! I don't want to get fleas!"

"Give it back, you thieving slut!" He seized the girl by the arm, but she broke away and dodged behind Corson.

"Ask *her* if I took it," she insisted, appealing to Corson. "She was watching me all the while."

"She's in league with you, then, but I'll have it out of you anyway!" He turned on Corson. "Just you try to stop me if you dare!"

"It's nothing to do with me!" Corson protested. "She's no friend of mine."

"You're a coward as well as a thief," he goaded. By now, all other pastimes at The Lame Fox had been abandoned, as people gathered 'round in hopes of a fight.

Corson was furious. Why did that little chit have to single her out to be her champion? Corson did not for a moment doubt that the girl was a pickpocket, but she was too proud to refuse a public challenge. Reluctantly, she got to her feet and faced her accuser.

"You've no sword," she said, and unsheathed her dagger instead. Though Corson was left-handed, she took the weapon in her right hand and wrapped her cloak carefully around her sword-arm.

He grinned and drew his own blade, also winding his cloak around his free arm as a shield. The crowd made room for them and there was a murmur of excited speculation. The wagering favored Corson.

The fighters circled warily, taking the measure of one another's speed and agility. Corson realized that her opponent was no mere tavern brawler—he handled himself too skillfully and responded too swiftly to her feints. He was in earnest, and she knew that she must either disarm him or kill him. But she couldn't risk coming before the city magistrates now.

For a moment she seemed to drop her guard, uncertain, and he lunged forward at once to press his advantage. But even as he closed in, Corson flung out her lowered left arm, freeing the furled cloak, and whipped it up across his face, blinding him. Without a pause she seized his wrist and twisted his arm back, kicking sharply into the side of his knee at the same time.

When he let his knife fall, Corson stepped on it firmly, then helped him to his feet. "Perhaps you've changed your mind," she suggested. He backed away, then turned and made for the door, shouldering his way through the jeering onlookers.

Corson kicked the knife away and the tavernkeeper picked it up, scowling at her. "Put up your blade," he ordered gruffly. "I won't have bloodshed in here."

Corson shrugged and sheathed her dagger. "It wasn't of my seeking. Why don't you keep a better watch on that harper of yours?"

He looked puzzled. "I keep no harper here."

"The singer," Corson insisted angrily, but the girl was nowhere to be seen. Corson felt she'd been made a fool of after all. She hurried out to the street, looking around for the singer. "When I find that little . . . !"

"I'm here," called a voice from across the way. Corson could just make out a slight figure, half hidden in the shadows of an alley. As she approached, the girl drew back out of sight and waited in a dark doorway.

"If you're that clumsy a pickpocket you'd better keep to your singing, curse you! I should wring your neck for dragging me into a fight with that madman. You owe me a share of the spoils for chasing him off."

The harper smiled. "I've a better offer to make you."

"I thought you might. But I don't need to take up with bungling pickpockets."

"I'm no thief, but I'm not a minstrel either. Come with me and I'll explain. I've a place not far from here."

"So you say. If you've anything to tell me you can say it right here."

"I don't arrange my affairs in the street. Follow me if you choose—I can give you a better meal than you'd get at the Fox." She started down the dark alleyway alone.

Corson hesitated, but her curiosity got the better of her suspicions. And the prospect of a good meal was hard to resist. She caught up with the girl and made her a mocking bow. "Corson brenn Torisk is at your service, milady!"

"And I'm Nick, of this city. Come, we're wasting time."
She led the way quickly through the narrow backstreets, but
before they'd gone far, Corson stopped and motioned her to
wait.

"He's following us, that fool! Whatever you stole from
him, he means to have it back."

"No matter, we're almost there—hurry!" She pulled Corson around a corner and unlocked the iron gate to a narrow,
two-story house.

Once they were safely inside, she lit two candles and offered one to Corson. "Wait for me upstairs. I'll bring us some
supper."

Corson was disappointed. So it was only a trick to rob her,
after all. No doubt there would be two or three of the girl's
confederates waiting upstairs. She shook her head and turned
back to the door. "I'll do without supper, thanks. The night's
yet young, you'll find another gull."

"It's no trap. Come, it's not likely I'd try that game with
you after seeing your skill at The Lame Fox. Shall I go up
ahead of you?"

"I'll see for myself," Corson muttered, unable as ever to
resist a dare. She climbed the stairs warily, ready for any
sudden attack, but when she reached the top she found herself
alone in a long, low-ceilinged room, dimly lit by a guttering
fire. She laid on another log, then lit the heavy silver candela-
bra that stood on the mantle and carried it with her as she
explored her surroundings. This was not the lodging of a petty
thief. A thickly woven, patterned carpet covered the floor, and
brocaded couches surrounded a table of dark, polished wood
inlaid with tiles. An open bookchest held several volumes,
and others lay about on the floor, the table and shelves.

The far wall was hidden by draperies, and Corson approached them suspiciously to see if they concealed a door.
She pushed aside the hangings quickly and found herself face
to face with a tall, menacing figure that reached out to seize
her arm. Corson had her sword in her hand before she realized
that the enemy was her own reflection.

She gazed at it in wonder. Mirrors were a luxury for the
wealthy, and Corson had never seen such a large sheet of
unlatticed glass. She was still marveling at the mirror's
ghostly mimicry when Nick's reflection appeared in the glass,

entering the doorway behind her. She was carrying a tray of food, and a lantern hung from her arm. Reluctantly, Corson turned from the mirror to join her at the table.

The meal was as good as promised. Her hostess set out a cold roast chicken and a round loaf of fresh white bread with a comb of honey. There was also a wedge of sharp cheese, some small yellow apples and a very costly wine.

As she ate, Corson was able to study her companion closely for the first time. She had changed her shabby clothing for a fur-trimmed robe, and she seemed a different person from the common tavern singer at The Lame Fox. She was very pale of complexion, with grey eyes and delicate, fine-boned features. Her black hair was close-cropped, revealing a high forehead and arched brows. Though a young woman, she was not the girl Corson had taken her for.

Corson gestured at her with a piece of bread. "If you're not a thief and you're not a minstrel, what are you? A whore?"

The woman laughed. "I told you I don't arrange my affairs in the street. I'm a scholar."

Corson looked about at the rich fittings of the chamber. "I see," she said in open disbelief. "And what would a scholar want with the likes of me?"

"I admired the way you dealt with that troublesome fellow at the Fox. A most impressive display of competence. It happens that I've need of a bodyguard just now."

Corson helped herself to more wine. "If you stayed away from places like The Lame Fox you wouldn't need a bodyguard, lady."

"But I only went there to hire a mercenary, you see. It's hardly a place I'd visit for amusement's sake. No, what troubles me is that my enemies are trying to have me murdered."

Corson stared at her for a moment. "Oh no," she said softly. "It's not fair; something like this always happens to me."

"You . . . ?"

"What did you say your name was? Nick? *Nyc?* Like *Nyctasia?*"

The woman rose hastily and backed a few paces towards the door. "Lady Nyctasia Selescq Rhaicime brenn Rhostshyl ar'n Edonaris," she said with a bow. "But we needn't be formal. *Please* don't get up."

Corson surveyed her defenseless quarry with contempt. *"You're* the dread sorceress who's slaughtered half the city with her spells?" She settled back more comfortably and finished her glass of wine.

"Unfortunately, my reputation for witchcraft is quite undeserved," Lady Nyctasia said wistfully. "If I'd half the powers folk credit me with, I'd not be in hiding now."

"There must be something to it. Do you know," Corson said with a winning smile, "that two different parties have hired me to kill you? Isn't that funny?"

"An amusing coincidence. My esteemed relations, no doubt, and the Teiryn clan?" She came over to the table and coolly refilled Corson's glass.

"They say that some of the Teiryns have died of a mysterious ailment lately. . . ."

"Mysterious! If the Teiryn didn't constantly intermarry, they could rid their line of that sickness for good and all, but they insist on keeping their estates within the family! This malady has been among them for centuries—it's all there in the city history. Anyone could have predicted that it would reappear. I *tried* to warn—" She paused. "This is the sort of thing that wins one a reputation for sorcery," she admitted.

"What of your own kin?" Corson demanded. "They'd like to be rid of you, too. And they paid handsomely for it." She had drawn her sword and was idly tracing patterns with it on the rug.

"Have a care, that carpet is valuable," Lady Nyctasia complained. She paced back and forth across the narrow room. "It's just a faction of my family that's after my blood, but a most powerful faction, led by the matriarch, Mhairestri. You see, I stand to inherit important titles and estates, and I've pledged my support to those who want a treaty with the Teiryns. That alone makes me a threat to Edonaris ambitions. Mhairestri would like to see my properties fall into more reliable hands."

"There's no more to it than that?" asked Corson, who was casually slicing pieces from an apple with her dagger. Her sword now lay close at her left hand.

"Oh, the list of my iniquities is endless, I assure you. I refused to marry my cousin Thierran though we'd been betrothed since childhood—that was an outrage. But the really unpardonable offense, I believe, was my treasonous view of the ancestral sovereignty of the Edonaris line. The city records show that the Teiryns' claims to power are at least as legitimate as our own." She paused in her pacing and picked up a brass candlestick. "Nobody appreciates a historian."

"I've been planning to make a long journey," she continued, "and I need an expert fighter like you as escort. You'd not lose by it—I'm one of the wealthiest people in the city." She waited for Corson's reply, armed only with the heavy candlestick.

Corson sighed. "You're a terrible disappointment to me, Lady. I was expecting something challenging, not a helpless little bookworm."

"Scholar."

"And I did need the money. . . ." Corson mused. "I want a better saddle. And a new pair of boots. I could make my fortune just by killing you."

"I daresay. But you'd not live to enjoy it. Mhairestri would never be so careless as to leave a living witness to my murder."

"She'd not be the first to try that trick," Corson said offhandedly. "But I appreciate the warning." She nibbled thoughtfully at a piece of cheese. "Do you suppose you're wealthy enough to better her offer *and* the Teiryns'?"

Lady Nyctasia relaxed visibly. She came up to Corson and fixed her with a critical gaze. "Oh, I think I can afford you a new pair of boots. And some decent clothing. A bath would not be amiss, either. I don't intend to travel with an unkempt sloven."

Corson grinned. "Don't forget the saddle, Your Ladyship."

"I forget very little, you'll find. I'm sure we can come to an agreement."

Corson raised her glass in a salute. "Your humble servant," she said, but Lady Nyctasia caught hold of her arm before she could take a drink.

"Corson, if you mean to remain in my service, you must really be more careful. You should have watched very closely when I poured your wine."

Corson stared at the goblet. "You viper! You tried to poison me!"

"I can't afford to leave anything to chance. *You* should

understand that. What's more, I've had a guard just outside the door all this while."

"Only one?" Corson scoffed. "I'd have killed the both of you."

"I know. That's why I didn't summon him before. Sandor!" she called. "Come in here!"

The guard entered at once, sword drawn. Then, seeing that Nyctasia was in no danger, he sheathed the weapon and bowed. "Yes, my lady . . . ?"

Corson started to her feet, speechless with outrage and disbelief. "You—!" she choked. It was the same man who'd fought with her at The Lame Fox.

2

NYCTASIA WAS SATISFIED with her arrangements. She'd provided for those of her servants whom she trusted, and the rest believed that she'd long since fled the city. That night she and Corson would slip out of Rhostshyl by a postern gate in the city walls. The sentry had been well paid to let them pass unchallenged. If it were another rainy, moonless night, all might yet be well.

She appeared confident and self-possessed, but inwardly Nyctasia was torn by warring passions. That she, an Edonaris, should be forced to slink through her own city like a common criminal, sneak out a back gate like a fugitive—! Though she opposed her family's pretensions to sole rule of Rhostshyl, yet strong ties of duty and heritage bound her to the ancestral home of the Edonaris. The city-state of Rhostshyl was governed by those members of the ruling families of the rank of Rhaicime, and Nyctasia should have been a strong voice on that council. Instead, she was an outcast, hunted from her home.

Though it was not by her own choice that she went into exile, she doubted the honesty of her own decision at times. Other duties claimed her—other desires drew her. She had long ago promised that someday she would join her lover, Erystalben ar'n Shiastred, in far-off Hlasven and there was no longer anything to be gained by waiting.

It was on her account he'd been driven from the city. Her family had been furious when she'd taken a lover from among the minor nobility and refused the husband chosen for her.

11

At first they had all but encouraged the connection, hoping that the Shiastred family would therefore take their part against the Teiryns, for Erystalben would one day be head of the House of Shiastred. Nyctasia's rebelliousness had not posed a serious threat until the unlooked-for death of her mother raised her suddenly to the rank of Rhaicime. It was then that the Edonaris became more insistent that she honor the marriage agreement that promised her to her cousin Thierran. They blamed Erystalben for her continued refusal, and he at last fled Rhostshyl rather than see his people incur the enmity of the most powerful family in the city. He had wanted Nyctasia to come with him, but while she had yet hoped to effect a conciliation between the rival families, she felt duty-bound to remain. Those hopes were shattered now and she would deny herself no longer.

Her reverie was broken by the shrill cry of a young beggar-child at her elbow, urging, "Alms, kind lady!"

She dropped a few coppers into his waiting hand, and looked him straight in the face. Accustomed to indifference even from charitable folk, the child was put on his guard at once.

"Who's following me?" Nyctasia asked.

Without seeming to look, the child gave a creditable description of Sandor.

"Is there no other behind him?"

"Oh, a younger one, lady? He's just come round the corner."

"Good. Now be off with you." Surprising the urchin with another coin worth more than the rest, she slipped into a narrow alleyway and let herself in to a dilapidated row-house. Nyctasia had rented houses in every quarter of the city, though she took care that the owners did not learn who their tenant was.

Sandor waited near the mouth of the alley. Before long, the other man passed by and hesitated, glancing down the passageway before he moved on.

"You won't find her that way, friend."

The stranger whirled round to face Sandor, who grinned knowingly and beckoned to him. "You're following the Lady Nyctasia," said Sandor. "Don't trouble to deny it. I've been after her all day myself, haven't you noticed? She came down this way and I know where she is now. I think we can be of help to each other, don't you?"

"What do you want of me?"

"Nothing more than you've been hired to do. It's two against one this way, easier for both of us. Once she's dead who's to say which of us did the deed? We'll both collect our pay."

"That's a bargain. Where is she?"

Sandor led him down the alley past the building Nyctasia had entered and stopped before an old, boarded-up house. "We've only to wait. There's no other way out."

They hid in a doorway across from the house. When Nyctasia did not appear, the youth grew more and more uneasy. "Where is she? What does she want in there? Are you sure—"

"Patience, my friend." Sandor took out a flask and tilted it to his lips. "Still green at this, eh?"

His companion flushed. "Give me some of that!"

Sandor laughed and passed the flask to him. "No need for haste, she's bound to come out soon. If you mean to live long at this trade you'd best learn to bide your time. Here, you've had enough of that—it's no drink for babes." He took back the flask and corked it, then caught the young man as he folded and fell.

3

"I've seen him before, but I can't think where," Nyctasia mused, looking down in some perplexity at the drugged youth. "Well, we'll soon find out." She crushed a few pungent leaves between her fingers and held them to his nose. After a moment he opened his eyes, choking.

"Teiryn or Edonaris?" Nyctasia demanded.

"Wha—?"

"Who sent you to kill me—the Teiryn or the Edonaris!"

He looked about him, still groggy, realizing that he was lying on a bench in a strange room. When he saw who it was who questioned him, he gasped and groped for his knife.

Sandor strode up, holding the missing knife as if it were a toy. "Her Ladyship asked you a question, man!"

The young man stared at him, then broke into a feeble laugh. "I should have heeded your advice, friend."

"What advice was that?" said Nyctasia.

"I told him he was too hasty by half, my lady. He's a raw one and no mistake."

"He must belong to the Teiryn, then. Only they'd hire such a bungler."

"I'm no hireling killer! I came to avenge Lord Rhavor on my own."

"Of course!" Nyctasia exclaimed. "Rhavor's servant—you were often with him of late." So that was how he'd known where she was likely to be found. She cursed herself for her carelessness. When she and Rhavor ar'n Teiryn had met in

14

secret, this fellow had been in attendance on him, yet she'd never given him a thought.

He was glaring at her. "I was with him the day you set your curse on him—just before he died! I heard you!"

"Then you merely heard me speaking to him. You must have heard any number of people speak to him that day. Why don't you kill all of them while you're about it?"

"You're the one did it. Everyone says so."

Nyctasia laughed. "My nurse used to say, 'If everyone tells you the sun's the moon, it will still be the sun.'"

"He died of the same curse as the rest of them!"

"Yes, he did. And Teiryns were dying of it long before I was born." She paused and said sadly, "Though your master might have lived years longer, if he'd not weakened himself with drink. Many's the time I tried to tell him it would be the death of him."

Rhavor's servant was puzzled by Lady Nyctasia's manner. Why should she deny the deed when she had him in her power? The words came back to him: "Rhavor, you'll be dead by first frost!" Could they have been meant, not as a threat, but a warning? He didn't believe her, yet somehow he was no longer afraid of her.

"You bewitched him," he muttered sullenly.

"Why is it," Nyctasia sighed, "that everyone believes my lies, but I can never persuade people of the truth?"

"Lady, if you let him go, he'll only come after you again," said Sandor.

Nyctasia looked defeated. Motioning Sandor aside, she said, "Lock him up downstairs and see that someone fetches him away after dark. Once I've reached safety, I'll send orders for his release. If you've anything to report, I'll be at the corner house till midnight. Stay at your post else."

"Very good, my lady." He bowed. "Good fortune await you, Lady Nyctasia."

"Farewell, Sandor." She crossed to the threshold of the next room, then paused. "Be careful," she said.

Nyctasia pushed aside the dark drapery curtaining the window and looked out across the city to where the last rays of the sun gilded the western towers of the Edonaris palace. For hundreds of years, its walls had witnessed the proud history of the Edonaris line. Ever since they had come to power in the city, the Edonaris had been known for their liberality and benevolence. They had been responsible for the elimination of slavery in Rhostshyl, and had tempered the harshness of the city laws in other ways as well. Thieves were no longer put to death in Rhostshyl, and many cities along the coast had followed this example. It was while the Edonaris dominated the Rhaicimate that Rhostshyl had entered the Maritime Alliance, benefiting from treaties of trade and mutual defense. The city had prospered and grown under their rule.

Nyctasia had always been proud of her name, but now she feared that this heritage had been betrayed. Though the Edonaris had come to power by lawful means, there were now those among them who would use any means to keep that power in their own hands. She was sure that it would not be the enmity of the Teiryn that destroyed her House, but the ruthless ambition of the matriarch Mhairestri and her supporters.

And yet she herself was not guiltless—she had been forced to take measures that repelled her, in order to counter her enemies. It had sickened her to learn what callousness she was capable of, what deceptions she would use, for her own ends. She had never thought to find herself taking prisoner a young fool like that—yet that was not the worst thing of which she accused herself.

Nyctasia leaned her head in her hands. She was resolved to put all that behind her and leave Rhostshyl while her spirit was still her own. She would be free of this madness! Erystalben needed her, and she could now do no good by remaining. With Rhavor's help, some compromise with the Teiryn might have been possible. But there was no one else among them who would listen to reason.

Rhavor had made no secret of his belief that his family's fanatical rivalry with the Edonaris was absolute folly. He had often held the feud up to ridicule. Nyctasia half smiled, remembering an encounter with the drunken Rhavor in Market Street. He had accosted her with a cheerful, "Ho! An Edonaris in my way! Cut her down, cut her down!" in blatant parody of his kinfolk.

Nyctasia had joined in the game: "A foul Teiryn! Have at you, miscreant!"

Waving their rapiers with exaggerated menace, they'd engaged in a ridiculous duel, parting with mock threats and laughter. How ironic that she was accused of his murder, when in truth she missed him sorely.

It was probably his own kin who killed him, she thought bitterly, though he'd plainly been set on destroying himself ever since the death of his wife. He had seemed to welcome the onset of the wasting sickness which cursed the Teiryn line, and had refused to husband his strength by abstaining from drink.

Lord Rhavor was already familiar to Nyctasia by reputation, when she'd first contrived to meet him at a tavern he was known to frequent. He'd not been long a widower, but Nyctasia was still a girl, and he'd been more amused than offended when she'd blurted out her plans for a marriage–alliance between them.

"My dear girl, not only am I twice your age, but I'm an ailing man as well. I'd soon make a widow of you."

Nyctasia flushed. "But, my lord, think what it could mean! If a Teiryn and an Edonaris should wed, there might be an end to this senseless feuding. Our families would be forced to come to terms!"

"Or to murder us both," he suggested with a smile. "You know as well as I that they're too caught up in their game to let a dying man and a child stand in their way." In truth, Lord Rhavor was not yet gravely ill. He spoke thus to discourage Nyctasia, but she would not be swayed from her purpose.

"Then you've nothing to lose, have you? And for my part, I am willing to take the risk."

"I believe you. But you're surely not of an age to marry without your family's consent, and I very much doubt that the Edonaris would think me a suitable match for you."

"I know all that," said Nyctasia impatiently. "I shall come of age in due course. But till then you must not take another wife—that's the gist of the matter!"

The mask of frivolity fell from Lord Rhavor's countenance. "I have no mind to marry again," he said coldly.

"That is all I ask," said Nyctasia, rising. "Forgive me. If the affair were not of such consequence, I should not intrude upon your grief." She tugged awkwardly at her sleeve for a moment. "Naturally I don't mean to take her place," she said stiffly. "I propose a political alliance. At least give some thought to my plan."

"Just as you like, Lady Nyctasia," he said indulgently. "We shall speak of it again when you come of age, if I live to see the day."

Lord Rhavor had many years yet to live, but when Nyctasia had reached her adulthood, he continued to oppose her plan. By then the illness had taken its toll and, though the remnants of his days meant little to him, he was reluctant to let Nyctasia risk her life for such a doubtful venture.

They continued to meet, however, and she'd still had hopes of persuading him, up to the time of his death. Now even that hope was gone.

Nyctasia let the curtain fall back, covering the window. Darkness had descended on the city, and the towers of the palace were lost from view.

4

NYCTASIA WAS ALARMED to see someone standing at the gate of the corner house. None of her people knew of this place save Sandor, and he wouldn't wait about outside. She was to meet Corson here soon, but it was a man who waited there—she could tell little more than that in the darkness.

She walked past the house without a glance or the slightest change in her stride. She was dressed in the shabby clothes and hooded cloak of a student, but the stranger was not fooled. "Lady Nyctasia!" he called after her, his voice low and urgent.

She immediately whirled around, crouched, her arms crossed over her chest, but the other made no move to throw a knife. He only stood in the shadows, waiting, watching her, motionless.

Nyctasia slowly stood and drew her sword. "Edonaris or Teiryn?" she said wearily. It was getting to be a habit.

"Neither the one nor the other, milady. A messenger. I bring you a letter."

"And why do you bring it here?"

"Such were the directions, my lady."

"Who gave you those directions?" she demanded.

"Milord Shiastred," was the answer.

Nyctasia's heart raced. She expected a letter at any time from Erystalben, and he could well have sent such a messenger as this. Yet her family knew about him. This letter might be a trap to draw her within arm's reach of a killer. Nyctasia

19

considered her own kinfolk much more dangerous than the Teiryns.

"Is an answer expected?" she said.

"A token, my lady, that His Lordship may know you received his message. A lock of milady's hair."

Nyctasia laughed. "'Ben doesn't know I've cut it. You'll have to take him this." Still keeping her distance, she tossed one of her gloves to the messenger.

"I'll leave this here, shall I, my lady?" he said quietly, reaching into his jacket. Nyctasia prepared to throw herself flat to the ground at the first glint of steel, but he drew out only a roll of paper and laid it on the gatepost, then bowed and walked off without waiting to be paid.

Nyctasia examined the letter by the dim starlight. The seal was indeed that of Shiastred and she tucked it inside her shirt, smiling at her own fears. Only Erystalben could have known to send a messenger here.

But then she heard footsteps close behind her and she hastily unlocked the gate and slipped inside the yard.

Someone peered at her through the palings. "Lady . . . ?"

"Corson! Good, come in." She hurried Corson inside and led the way upstairs.

Corson sprawled on a couch without waiting for permission to sit. She knew that there was nothing Lady Nyctasia could do about her impertinence and she meant to take full advantage of her position. "Are you ready to go?" she asked curtly.

Nyctasia paced the room restlessly. "I've been ready to leave for a long time."

"You know, if the gate sentries have guessed who you are, it may yet come to a fight. Are you of any use with that sword?" She eyed Nyctasia's rapier doubtfully.

"I'm not a professional murderer, of course, but I've trained with the best fencers at court."

Corson groaned. "Fencing! This isn't a duel, Your Ladyship. I only hope your horses are as good as you claim. Our best chance is in surprise and speed."

"My stables have the fastest horses in the city," she said proudly. "Most people don't understand the principles of breeding. But it's simply—"

"Can you *ride* them?" Corson interrupted.

"There are not many beside myself who can," Nyctasia said with dignity.

Corson looked glum. It was hard to picture the Lady Nyctasia doing anything more strenuous than plucking a harp. It would be so much simpler just to kill her and collect the blood money.

Nyctasia leaned against the back of a chair and looked searchingly at Corson. "I hope you've no weakness for gambling. Your face betrays your every thought."

"I always lose," Corson admitted. "And this looks to be a losing game as well." She badly wanted a drink.

"Maybe so. But you'll find me a safer wager than Lady Mhairestri."

Wine and water had been set out, but Corson was wary of Lady Nyctasia's hospitality. "We'll just have to trust one another, then. Let's drink a toast to that, shall we?" She poured out the wine and handed a cup to Nyctasia. "After you, my lady."

"I don't drink spirits," Nyctasia demurred.

"Please, I insist," said Corson grimly, her hand on her sword hilt.

Nyctasia laughed. "Well, perhaps the occasion does warrant some special observation." She raised her glass. "To the success of our venture."

Corson watched her swallow the wine before reaching for her own cup. "To trust and good faith," she said.

Nyctasia sat down across from her and drew out the unopened letter. As she broke the seal, she thought again of the unknown messenger. "Corson, did you pass anyone at the corner?"

"No, but I saw Sandor crossing the thoroughfare. I don't think he saw me."

"Sandor? He should be in Westgate Street by now."

"He was coming this way."

Nyctasia frowned. Something must be wrong. Her suspicions grew sharper—was Corson herself the danger? "I'll go down to meet him."

"By yourself?"

"He may want to speak to me alone." She stood. "I'll be back directly. We have to start out soon, it's nearly midnight."

As soon as she heard Nyctasia leave the house, Corson hurried to the far wall and drew back the heavy draperies. Ever since she'd discovered the great mirror she'd been longing for another chance to study her reflection.

Nyctasia could see Sandor lying in the street, not far from the gate. Pulling back the bolt at once she hastened to him, and knelt over the still form, searching for any sign of life— but the man was dead. Before she could rise she was seized roughly from behind and dragged into an alleyway, a knife at her throat.

A second assailant stood before her, smiling, his sword ready. "I don't believe I've ever seen you at such a loss for words, 'Tasia," he said. "You needn't feel abashed. It took me some time to find you out, though of course I never believed the rumors that you'd already fled the city. Rumors which you no doubt encouraged."

"I started them," Nyctasia whispered. "But I can be gone by morning. Let me go and the family will never be troubled by me again, I swear it!"

He laughed. "I intend to see that the family is not troubled further by you, my dear cousin. I'm well aware of your plans, but I'm afraid they'll have to be altered. Think yourself fortunate that I found you before the Teiryns."

"Listen to me, Thierran—" Nyctasia began.

"Don't waste words with her!" the other man broke in, and Nyctasia recognized the voice of Mescrisdan, Lord Thierran's brother. "She'll keep us talking here 'til dawn. I say kill her and have done with it." Suddenly he gasped, and Nyctasia felt his grip slacken. She broke free, dodging to the side, and saw him fall as Corson wrenched her broadsword from his back.

Corson met the other man's attack with cold precision. She turned aside his blade and followed through with a thrust that tore his arm to the bone. The sword dropped from his grasp and he made a frantic lunge to retrieve it, but Corson dealt him a sharp blow across the back of his neck with her free hand. As he fell to the ground Nyctasia snatched the sword from his reach.

Dazed, he tried to crawl toward Nyctasia, his wounded arm hanging limp and useless. Corson kicked him onto his back, looming over him in the narrow alleyway. "No!" he cried. "Please...."

"Corson, don't!" gasped Nyctasia.

Corson put up her sword. "Next time remember to guard against attack from the *left* hand," she advised him. Her boot caught him under the jaw and he lay as still as his companion.

They carried the bodies into the courtyard, and for the first time Corson could see that the two men who'd attacked Nyctasia were identical. "There have always been twins in my family," Nyctasia said, noticing Corson's stare.

"Do you have a double, too?" Corson asked suspiciously. Perhaps this wasn't the singer after all.

"I've often wished I did—it might have been useful. But there won't even be one of me if we're not gone from here soon."

Nyctasia paused for a moment to look down at the still form of Thierran ar'n Edonaris. "He's hated me ever since I refused to marry him," she remarked.

5

AT THAT HOUR of the night the streets were usually empty, save for noisy drunkards and silent thieves. Yet they soon realized that someone was following them on horseback.

"Do you have any of your people behind us?" Corson asked.

"Yes, but they're on foot," Nyctasia said worriedly.

They passed a group of shouting roisterers, and Corson suddenly joined in the uproar, singing as loudly as any of them:

> "I once knew a soldier
>   so skilled with his sword
>   that they sued for his service,
>   both lady and lord!"

Nyctasia clutched at her arm. "Are you mad?!"

"I'm being inconspicuous. Sober folk wouldn't ride out this late.

> "I once knew a fisher
>   so skilled with her net
>   there was nary a fish
>   that the wench couldn't get!"

she roared.

Nyctasia had to acknowledge the sense in this. Silence might be suspect. She resigned herself to Corson's performance.

Without warning, a figure lunged at them from a nearby doorway, and they both reached for their weapons in alarm. "Get out of here, you sotted curs!" screamed a large man in a nightshirt. "Decent folk are trying to sleep!"

"All right, we'll go," Corson said hastily, but he had already seen their half-drawn swords.

"Threaten an unarmed citizen, will you, you vermin," he shouted after them. "Warder! Arrest those cutthroats!"

The rider behind them broke into a trot, and they realized that they'd been followed by an officer of the night watch. Nyctasia suddenly turned her horse and started back before Corson could stop her. "I'll show you who's vermin," she muttered.

Corson was aghast. She caught up with Nyctasia and grabbed her bridle. "What are you doing?!"

"I'm being inconspicuous. Do you want the City Guard chasing us through the streets?"

The watchman rode up to them. "What's the matter here?"

"We—" Corson began, but her horse suddenly swerved to the side and reared, as Nyctasia surreptitiously jabbed her spur into its flank.

"Good evening, warder," she said in her haughtiest tone. "I'm afraid my servant has had too much to drink." She sounded bored and annoyed, and her bearing proclaimed her a personage of the highest station. It was too dark for him to see how poorly she was dressed, and she kept her face well back in her hood.

"Ah, forgive me, Your Ladyship," the guardsman said anxiously. "There was a complaint, but I'm sure . . ."

"I'm not drunk," Corson protested, swaying in her saddle.

"Be still!" Nyctasia ordered. "I'll see that she doesn't bother anyone else, warder. I don't recall the fine for causing a public disturbance, but I'm sure this will suffice." She pressed a few heavy coins into his hand.

He bowed. "Certainly—thank you, Your Ladyship. If you should require an escort . . ."

"No need," said Nyctasia indifferently. "I assure you she'll be disciplined for this." She turned away, leading Corson's horse by the bridle.

"Come along," she snapped.

Corson swayed again and leaned in closer to Nyctasia. "As

soon as I have the chance, I'm going to slit your throat."

"Wits may be a sharper weapon than any sword," said Nyctasia with a smug smile.

As they approached the gate, Nyctasia hugged the wall, keeping to the shadow of the watchtower. She watched the quiet streets for signs of danger as Corson rode ahead to meet the sentry.

Corson dismounted and handed the woman a pouch, then helped her to pull back the heavy bolts. They both pushed their weight against the gate, and the guard in the watchtower paid no heed as the portal slowly swung outward.

Only then did Nyctasia emerge from the shadows and follow Corson through the narrow gap that opened onto a rough pasture track. By the time the gate had been shut behind them, they were halfway across the field.

Looking over her shoulder, Corson was not surprised to see the bright flash of a lantern from the sentry tower. "Arm yourself!" she shouted to Nyctasia. "They've signaled someone—make for the forest!"

Soon they heard hoofbeats behind them, echoing their own. But Nyctasia's horses were all she'd claimed, and they'd put a good distance between themselves and their pursuers when a second band of riders broke from the cover of the forest just in front of them.

"Ride that way," Corson called, "divide them." Nyctasia swerved to the right, spurring her mount to even greater efforts. Corson fell back, trying to draw the enemy after her, but two of them broke away and followed Nyctasia.

For a time, Nyctasia led them a hard chase, but they were too close upon her to be outdistanced. The ground was uneven, broken by small hills and ravines—good grazing land but unsuited for galloping horses. Her mount plunged down a slope and easily leapt the swollen stream, but as it tried to scramble up the steep embankment on the other side, it could find no footing in the slippery mud. It slid back twice, then balked at a third attempt. Nyctasia had no time to urge it on before one of her pursuers was upon her.

She turned to attack, but her blow glanced harmlessly off the other's shield. He quickly thrust in beneath her upraised arm to pierce the light chain mail over her ribs. Doubling over with a cry, she fell from the saddle onto the soft mud of the bank and lay motionless as her horse nuzzled her shoulder, nickering softly.

The man dismounted and approached her cautiously. Her sword lay unsought by her open hand, and he stepped firmly on the haft as he bent down to look at her.

Nyctasia's dagger lashed out wildly, barely scratching his hand, but a burning pain seared through his arm, leaving it numb. In moments, the poison reached his heart, and he was dead before he fell to the ground.

Nyctasia dragged herself into the stream, hoping the cold water would slow her bleeding. On the crest of the slope above her, two riders clashed and she saw one of them knock the sword from the other's grip. As the disarmed warrior turned to flee, Nyctasia raised herself on one elbow and screamed, "Corson! This way!"

Corson hesitated, anxious to give chase, but instead she leapt from her horse and clambered down the embankment. Nyctasia struggled to rise, clutching at her side. She gave a hiss of pain as Corson grabbed her under the arm and pulled her upright.

"Can you ride?" Corson demanded brusquely. Without waiting for an answer, she led over Nyctasia's horse and helped her to mount. "No matter. Just keep your seat, I'm warning you. If you fall off, I'll leave you behind."

Nyctasia leaned against the animal's neck and moaned. "Vicious bitch," she said faintly, but she held on as Corson seized the reins and led the way to level ground.

They reached the forest unchallenged and rode in stony silence for some time before Nyctasia sat up and took the reins. "Corson, you must be a demon in battle. There were at least a score of swords after us—how many of them did you kill?!"

Corson considered. "It's hard to say to a certainty, but not more than four, I should think."

"But what became of the rest?"

"The sentry must have taken her story to both parties. Don't you see?" Corson started to laugh. "The Teiryns and the Edonaris *both* had their henchmen waiting to waylay you—

and when they met, they started warring between themselves. They're so busy slaughtering each other back there that they've forgotten about us. Isn't that funny?"

"It is indeed," said Nyctasia. But it hurt to laugh.

6

"HLANN ASYE, BUT that hurts!" They had ridden till dawn, then made camp by a stream where Nyctasia was bathing her wounded side.

"You were lucky. I thought it was worse than that."

"I'm known for my luck," Nyctasia said with a grimace. She cut a strip of cloth from the hem of her shirt and bound the wound tightly, cursing like a peasant.

Corson was surprised to hear her swear by the name of Asye, the deity of the common people. Most of the nobility and the educated considered the worship of Asye a vulgar superstition, and professed belief only in the Indwelling Spirit —the *vahn*.

"You're a follower of the Hlann?" Corson asked curiously. It was an old word meaning either "Lady" or "Lord," but it was used now only for the androgynous Asye.

The Lady Nyctasia looked embarrassed. "Oh, when I was younger, mainly to annoy my family. Oaths are just habit. Folk wouldn't use the name of Asye so freely if they really believed." As if to herself, she added, "and it's not always those who swear by the *vahn* who believe in it.

"But aren't you hungry, Corson?" Nyctasia changed the subject deliberately. "'Feed the flesh and the spirit thrives,' you know."

This was one proverb with which Corson wholeheartedly agreed. Their saddlebags were packed with smoked meat, bread, dried fruit, and cheese. "I brought along a flask of wine for you, since you have such a taste for it," Nyctasia said. "It's in my satchel, there."

Corson pulled over the bag and rummaged through it impatiently, pushing aside some leatherbound books which were locked with clasps.

"Be careful with those books! No, that's ink—the *other* flask." Corson uncorked the wine, but then hesitated. "It's not poisoned," laughed Nyctasia.

"It might make me sleepy. I have to keep watch."

"Do you want me to drink some first?" Nyctasia asked provokingly.

Scowling, Corson shoved the flask back into the satchel, dislodging the clasp on one of the books. To spite Nyctasia, she picked it up and opened it, but the writing baffled her. "This is gibberish!"

"It's Old Eswraine, a dead language—the mother tongue of the languages of the coastal countries. That's why they're all so much alike, and—" she paused in her explanation. "But do you know how to read?"

Corson was not insulted by the question. People of her station were rarely literate. "I traveled about with a student when I was first out of the army. We traded lessons in swordplay for lessons in letters, but I think I got the better of the bargain—he'd never have made a swordsman. I've never met a scholar yet who was good for anything much," she added pointedly.

"What a shame that you didn't learn any manners while you were about it," Nyctasia remarked with a yawn. She pillowed her head on a saddlebag and pulled her cloak over her. "Good night . . . if you still want to cut my throat, this is your chance." She did not really expect to sleep, oppressed as she was with fear and uncertainty, but her weariness soon overcame her.

She dreamt that Lady Mhairestri had sent for her. The matriarch had refused to see her for months, and Nyctasia was certain that at least one of the attempts on her life had been carried out at Mhairestri's behest, yet she did not hesitate to obey the old woman's summons. Though Nyctasia might defy her wishes, she would never show her the slightest disrespect. Lady Mhairestri rarely left her own apartments. She re-

ceived Nyctasia in her bedchamber, seated stiffly upright by
the fire, her face hard and forbidding. Nyctasia dropped to one
knee before her and formally kissed her hand, but when she
raised her head she found herself facing a stranger. This aged
lady only resembled the matriarch.

She looked down at Nyctasia kindly and said, "Truly it is
remarkable, child. You could be one of my own daughters."

Bewildered and grateful, Nyctasia leaned her forehead
against the old woman's knee. "I wish that I could," she said
earnestly.

"But you must not stay here. You are in danger."

Nyctasia realized suddenly that this was so. She had to get
away at once, yet she did not rise. "You will give me your
blessing, Mother, before I go?" she whispered, bowing her
head again, humbly.

The old woman touched Nyctasia's hair lightly with one
frail hand, murmuring a ceremonial phrase, then said, "Now
you must be gone, child," and pushed her away with surprising strength.

Nyctasia looked up, startled, and it was Mhairestri she saw
glaring at her, furious, hand raised to strike again. "Get out!"
said the matriarch in a low, harsh voice. She hit at Nyctasia's
face and arms. "Get out of here!"

Corson was shaking her. "Get up! We have to get out of
here!"

7

"WAKE UP!" CORSON whispered. "There's someone coming."

"Who . . . ?" Nyctasia peered around vaguely, yawning. She sneezed.

"Be quiet, they'll find us—hurry!" But before they could reach their horses, an arrow flew past them. Corson dropped to the ground at once, pulling Nyctasia down with her.

"They've found us."

A group of ragged figures, with daggers and shortswords drawn, came from among the trees and formed a circle around them. Corson and Nyctasia slowly got to their feet, looking around for any avenue of escape. They were trapped.

But as Nyctasia hopelessly surveyed their captors, she found not a Teiryn or an Edonaris crest among them, and she suddenly laughed aloud, almost giddy with relief. These were not the hirelings of her enemies, but only common robbers!

One of the thieves stepped forward and looked at her quizzically. "Do we amuse you?"

"Please forgive my incivility," Nyctasia said. "I was only thinking of the old saying, you know, that the penniless don't fear thieves." She gestured at her own shabby garments. *"I* certainly have nothing to fear."

The thief looked them over scornfully. With her patched cloak and satchel of books, Nyctasia was the picture of a wandering student, and Corson looked the vagabond soldier that she was.

"Yet you have such fine horses—stolen I'd say from the

look of you two." He shook his head disapprovingly. "Get their weapons," he ordered.

"You'd better decide how badly you want them," Corson said grimly. "How many of your people can you spare?" She held her broadsword ready. Corson would give up her goods if she must, but would not let herself be disarmed without a fight. "Our swords aren't worth what they'll cost you."

"She's in a terrible humor," Nyctasia remarked. "She killed four people in a skirmish outside Rhostshyl last night. As a matter of fact, that's how we got the horses."

"This city's getting too dangerous," said the thief. He shrugged. "All right, don't get their weapons—but you'll put up that sword if you want to keep it." When Corson had reluctantly obeyed, he walked over to inspect the saddlebags. "Books," he muttered, tossing them out on the ground.

Nyctasia winced. "Is there no respect for learning anymore?" she asked plaintively.

"Students are thieves' bane," he sneered. "They never have anything worth stealing." He turned to Corson. "But *you* might have picked up some loot. Throw that pouch over here."

Corson cursed. "Someday I'll make you pay for this. I swear it." She tossed her purse at the robber's feet.

He shook it with satisfaction. "We'll have the jewelry, too. You, Nessa—"

One of his followers approached them, hand outstretched. Nyctasia surrendered her belongings with indifference. She was carrying nothing of value.

"Copper," complained Nessa, pocketing Nyctasia's earrings. "Ho, but look at *these* now—gold, or I'm a fishmonger!"

Corson seethed with frustrated rage. Her golden earrings were her most treasured possession. The ringleader held them up and peered at them, delighted. "You're right. These will fetch a good price. And soldiers are usually such poor game, too. What they don't spend on drink they throw away at dicing. You give me new respect for the breed," he said to Corson.

Suddenly her sword was in her hand again. She gripped the hilt so tightly that her arm shook. "Get out of here, you scum, before I forget what the odds are!"

The thieves laughed. "We don't want to tangle with her," one of them shouted, "she killed four people at Rhostshyl!"

"I don't see any of you bravos trying to disarm her," Nyctasia said quietly. "Bear-baiting is cowards' sport." She turned to the leader. "Why don't you call them off before it's too late? You have what you want."

The robber grinned and casually put on Corson's earrings. "We'd better go while we still can, eh?" He made a sign for his people to withdraw. "Come on, bravos," he said.

Corson slowly lowered her sword. Her whole body was trembling. She watched as Nyctasia gathered up her books, inspecting them for damage. "What do you want with those useless things now?" she shouted. "They took everything— our horses, our money . . . I'll kill someone for this! *Me*, robbed!"

Nyctasia looked at her warily. "Never mind, I'll make good your losses. I have a fortune in keeping at Chiastelm."

"And how do you think we'll get there without horses?"

Nyctasia shrugged. "We'll get there, don't worry."

"Well, what do you mean to do?!"

"To begin with, I think I'll take a bath. I'm filthy."

"A bath!"

But Nyctasia was already walking downstream towards a pool that was hidden among the trees. Best to leave Corson alone to nurse her wounded pride. "That's right, a bath," she called back. "It's a habit among civilized people. I won't be long."

Uneasily, Corson watched her move out of sight. She knew that she should stay with Lady Nyctasia, but she was glad of a chance to recover her temper alone. "Stay within earshot," she called, and leaned back against a tree, clenching and unclenching her fists. She felt more exhausted than after an actual fight.

She could hear the Lady Nyctasia singing to herself as she bathed. She'd just lost her horses and goods, and the silly bitch was singing!

> "So beware, my Lady Alys,
> This is a haunted palace . . ."

Her voice was high and pure and serene.

Corson liked the Ballad of Mad Alys. When it ended, she called to Nyctasia, "You're crazy, Lady, you really are!"

"All the Edonaris are crazy," Nyctasia answered, amused. "And all the Teiryn are stupid. That's what folk say in Rhostshyl, among themselves. Do you know what I most regret leaving behind? My harp."

"If you'd brought it, those rutting bandits would have stolen it."

"That's true." She began to sing "The Queen of Barre."

A bath would feel good at that, Corson reflected.

Nyctasia was kneeling by the water, half-dressed, drying her hair with the corner of her cloak. She did not hear Corson's step on the soft moss bordering the pool. By the time she realized that Corson was standing over her, it was too late to conceal her side, smoothly healed, where there had been a vicious wound the night before. For a moment they stared at one another, frozen.

"So your reputation for witchcraft is quite undeserved," Corson said coldly. "You heal quickly for someone who's not a witch!"

"I lied. I'm an excellent liar."

"I've noticed that about you. What other lies have you told me, sorceress?"

Nyctasia began rubbing at her hair again, trying to appear calm. "I don't really remember," she said carelessly. "No doubt I said whatever was necessary. I always do." She did not rise to her feet, hoping that Corson would not kill someone who was unarmed and on her knees.

"You *did* put a curse on the Teiryns. You brought the sickness on them!"

"Don't be a fool!"

"If you can heal with magic, you can kill with it."

"That isn't so!" Nyctasia exclaimed earnestly. "Healing is much simpler. I can explain—"

"Liar! I should just bring your head back to Rhostshyl and collect my wages!"

"You can't be stupid enough to believe that I could be driven out of my own city if I had that kind of power! Why would I need to lie to you—why would I need you at all—if I could defend myself with spells?!"

"You make everything sound true, but you'll not get around me again with your clever words. If I see you again, you'd better have some spells to defend yourself with!" She turned and strode off furiously, without a backward glance at the dread sorceress of Rhostshyl.

When Corson was out of sight, Nyctasia slowly stood and finished dressing, her hands trembling at the memory of Corson's barely restrained fury. The danger just passed made her think of an experience she had long tried to forget. Years ago, she had led the hunt for a savage wildcat which had killed a herdsman on one of her estates. In the end, it had broken free of the hounds and tried to spring at her—but she had only been waiting for a clear shot and she sent an arrow cleanly through its throat.

Nyctasia had been in at the kill on many dangerous hunts since then, but she still sometimes dreamt of the cat at bay, and the wild hatred in its eyes as it crouched to spring at her. Corson had turned on her with the same look of desperate rage.

"But it's my own carelessness that will kill me," Nyctasia thought. She was furious with herself for allowing Corson to learn the truth just then, while still smarting from her humiliating defeat by the thieves. Nyctasia could not afford to be careless, and she never forgave herself for a mistake.

She doubted that she could reach Chiastelm alone, but there was nothing to do now but wait. Corson might return when she'd come to her senses. If she hadn't carried out her threats then, at the height of her fury, she wouldn't do so later in cold blood. Corson was no fool, thank Asye!

Nyctasia gathered some dry twigs for kindling and began to stir up the dying campfire. She was at home in the woods. Like any aristocrat, she'd been thoroughly trained in the hunt as well as the other courtly arts of fencing, dancing, harping, and etiquette. Hunting and harping she enjoyed; she was adequate at the rest.

If only she had her bow now, she could at least hunt some small game for dinner—but it was hanging from the saddle of her stolen horse. With a sigh, she settled herself comfortably

at the foot of a tree and drew out the letter from Erystalben
ar'n Shiastred, still unread.

". . . So I've the Teiryn to thank that you remember your
word to me at last. If I could not draw you from your beloved
city, at least those fools can drive you from it. 'Tasia, that
adder's nest is not worth your regrets. Let it look to its own
destruction. Your place is here. I have carried out much of our
purpose, but it will go for nothing unless you soon join your
power to mine.

"I've seen no further sign of Vhar Kastenid, though I do
not believe he has given up the battle. But together we will be
able to hold this place against any enemy. Come to me
quickly, 'Tasia. At times I do fear that you have forgotten.
And then I do not see my way clearly. . . ."

Nyctasia read on to the end of the letter, then put it away,
smiling to herself. She had never forgotten, not for a moment.
It was true that she could not leave the city as easily as Erystalben had—an Edonaris had duties which could not be abandoned lightly. And she had left behind much that she loved.
But she did not regret.

* * *

Corson walked blindly for a time, trying not to think of the
way she'd been shamed before the Lady Nyctasia. But again
and again she saw the thieves gloating over their spoils,
laughing at her. The thought of her own helplessness sickened
her, and she finally stopped in a small clearing to rest. Her
hands were scratched from heedlessly pushing her way
through thorn bushes, and twigs and brambles clung to her
sleeves.

She sat with her knees drawn up to her chin and brooded
over her past defeats and present losses. Painful memories
assailed her of every time she'd been beaten, outnumbered,
humiliated. Unwillingly, she remembered being captured in
battle and led through the streets with the other prisoners, her
hands tied behind her. The wounds from that war had long
since been healed, but Corson had never recovered from the
disgrace.

She lay her head on her arms, cursing wearily. If she could only get drunk, she thought, she could forget everything. She licked her lips. "I don't even have any water. I should have kept to the stream. It's that witch's fault . . . I hope they find her and butcher her!" ·

Corson frowned. She couldn't decide what to make of the Lady Nyctasia. The woman had admitted to practicing magic, but she'd fled from Rhostshyl nevertheless, and Corson had seen her defenseless before swords. Clearly she had no power to strike down her enemies at will, but could she cast spells to waste them with a sickness? And was she even now working magic against Corson herself?

"Spells!" she spat. "I'll go back and settle this affair with her one way or another!" She'd agreed to escort Lady Nyctasia to Chiastelm and it might after all be the wiser course to keep her in sight. And then perhaps she could still collect the rest of her fee. . . .

Yet Corson remained where she was, uncertain, as the dusk gradually deepened around her. She still had made no move to rise when she suddenly heard the sound of approaching horses. In a moment she had leapt to her feet and hidden herself in the shadows.

"If they're robbers they're too late," she thought, gripping her sword hilt, "and if they're not, maybe I can rob them and get myself a horse." She waited, sword in hand, till a rider came into view, but then she only stood where she was, open-mouthed and staring.

Nyctasia was riding her own horse and leading Corson's. "I told you we'd get to Chiastelm somehow," she said.

8

"HOW DID YOU get those horses back?!"

Nyctasia grinned. "I destroyed the entire band of thieves with my murderous magic arts, of course. Have you forgotten that I'm an all-powerful enchantress?"

Corson sheathed her sword, not trusting to her own temper. "Answer me!"

"Take care you don't arouse my wrath, woman. You know I might change you into a mushroom and eat you."

Corson started towards her. If she had to beat an answer out of this lying witch, she was quite prepared to do it. "You cursed, japing—"

Nyctasia backed her horse away a few paces into the brush. "Very well, I'll explain about the horses," she laughed, "but you won't like it."

"I know," said Corson, grabbing for Nyctasia's bridle. The horse shied back suddenly, kicking out, and Corson pitched forward into the brambles. They tore at her neck as she tried to rise, and thorns caught fast in her hair.

"Corson? Are you hurt?" Nyctasia dismounted and pushed her way through the thicket.

Corson glared at her and tried to pull free from the entangling branches, cursing as the briars raked her fingers. Nyctasia could see that she would have to be handled carefully. She was in no temper to be reasoned with—but reason was not the only form of persuasion.

She smiled to herself. "You're making it worse. Here, let me help." She knelt beside Corson and began to unsnarl her hair. There was a great deal more of it than she'd expected. "The braid's come down. I think I'll have to cut it off," she teased.

Corson struck at her halfheartedly. "If you *dare* . . . !"

"Hold still." Nyctasia carefully undid the thick braid, freeing loose strands of hair from around the thorns. "There, now."

"Are you finished?"

"Not quite." She combed her fingers through the heavy waves of waist-length hair. "I wish I had a brush."

"I'll do it," said Corson. She pulled her hair over one shoulder to braid it.

Nyctasia touched a finger lightly to the back of her neck. "You're bleeding."

"I suppose you're a vampire as well as a witch."

Nyctasia leaned over and nibbled at Corson's throat. "Mmm—hmm."

"What are you doing?!"

"I'm casting a spell on you. Don't be afraid." She laughed softly and brushed her lips along Corson's jaw.

Corson was stunned. Lady Nyctasia was a client, an aristocrat, an arrogant, lying, sorcerous—

Nyctasia kissed her again, on the mouth, and started unlacing her tunic.

"But you . . . you . . ." stammered Corson, "I. . . ."

"What's wrong?" Nyctasia breathed, close to her ear.

Corson couldn't remember. She would worry about it later, she decided. Abandoning her misgivings, she let Nyctasia push her to the ground.

Nyctasia straddled her, laughing. She spread open the tunic and slowly slid it down over Corson's shoulders, then stretched her body over Corson's and gently kissed her eyelids and the corners of her mouth.

Corson raised her shoulders and tried to shrug out of the sleeves. "I can't move."

"Good," said Nyctasia, sliding her small scholar's hands up beneath the loose chain-mail.

"Oh," Corson said faintly, and fell back onto the grass. Nyctasia lay over her and buried her face in the deep mass of hair at the base of Corson's neck. She nuzzled her ear. "Now aren't you glad you didn't kill me?" she whispered.

* * *

Corson was ordinarily a light sleeper, but it was well into the next morning before she woke, and then she lay for some time with one arm flung over her eyes, trying to think of something to say to Lady Nyctasia. She could hear her moving about the clearing, building up the fire.

Then Nyctasia stood over her. "Ho, bodyguard, wake up! You're supposed to be protecting me from the dangers of the forest, aren't you? Wild beasts. Enemies. And robbers," she added maliciously.

Corson sat up quickly and glowered at her. "What chance did I have against twenty people?"

"None at all, but you're almost foolhardy enough to try it. You certainly had me worried." She shook her head and wandered back to the fire to check on the spitted bird she'd shot that morning.

Corson shook the twigs and leaves from her hair then hastily braided it and bound it up before joining her companion. She was ravenous. "All right," she said, "how *did* you get the horses back?"

Nyctasia looked up from turning the makeshift spit. "I once told you that I bred those horses myself. Well, I didn't breed them just for swiftness. If they're taken they'll return to me—you can see how they've chewed through their ropes. If any of those thieves tried to stop them they were probably trampled to death. Thoroughbreds can be quite vicious."

Corson smiled, cheered at the thought of the bandits' undoing. "That bird smells good."

Nyctasia had slit the skin and stuck in pieces of wild garlic, then stuffed the cavity around the spit with aromatic grasses. "When I took up the study of herb lore, I little thought of such homely arts as this," she said, "but I've found it most useful for seasoning game."

"I can guess why you studied such things, Lady," Corson muttered. "You breed horses no one can steal, you heal wounds overnight, why can't you use your powers to defend yourself?"

"Corson, it took me years to breed those horses. I had to lay spells on four generations of the bloodline before it produced the traits I wanted. Most magic requires long, painstaking preparation, like anything else—it's of no use for felling one's enemies at a moment's notice. There isn't time!"

"But you had time enough to lay spells on the Teiryn family."

Nyctasia laughed. "I suppose I *could* breed a fatal disease into the Teiryn line, but, don't you see, I'd need their complete cooperation to do it. The Teiryn may be stupid, but they're not horses. Besides, I tried to tell you before—it's far more difficult to kill with magic than to heal. The reason is perfectly plain if you consider the matter . . ." Nyctasia's voice had taken on an ardent, lecturing tone which Corson was beginning to recognize.

"I knew I'd be sorry I asked for this explanation," she said, yawning.

Nyctasia ignored her. "The body naturally desires to mend itself. A healing spell only has to enhance inclinations that are already present—there's no *resistance*. Whereas, in order to *afflict*—"

"Enough! I see!" Corson interrupted. "And I'll wager you could tell me the contrary and make it seem just as convincing." Her opinion was more or less that if Lady Nyctasia were telling the whole truth, then she, Corson, was Empress of Liruvath. "What I want to know," she continued, "is, were you lying about that money of yours in Chiastelm?"

For a moment, Nyctasia was profoundly shocked and outraged. To be accused of murder and sorcerous evildoing was unfortunate, but to be suspected of a vulgar and base deception was an insufferable affront to her honor. An Edonaris might poison an enemy, if it were expedient, but would never stoop to cheating on a debt. Nyctasia had fought duels over lesser insults, but there was no way to demand satisfaction from a professional swordswoman like Corson.

She gazed into the fire, silent, until she had mastered her indignation, then said reprovingly, "I am an Edonaris."

"You are a liar! An excellent liar, if I remember rightly."

"Not where my honor is concerned. You'll be paid for your services, never fear."

Corson bowed. "Pray forgive my offense, Your Ladyship, but I've never before served a noblewoman who played the minstrel in a tavern, or cursed by Asye, either. If you don't respect your own rank, how should I?"

Despite herself, Nyctasia could not keep back a smile. "*I've* never before had a guard as ready with her tongue as

with her sword. Consider yourself fortunate that a lady doesn't
lower herself to duel with a social inferior!"

"Oh, I do," snorted Corson, "very fortunate. Let's eat."

* * *

They concluded their plans as they approached the port
town of Chiastelm. "We'd best settle our accounts first," said
Nyctasia. "I know you're anxious about your money. I do
business with a reliable moneychanger on Market Street—we
can go there straightaway." She paused. "I want to take a
cargo ship out of port tonight, but I'd rather the crew didn't
see me before we sail. Can you arrange passage for me?"

"Gladly. But how will I get word to you? Where will you
be hiding?"

"I own property just outside of town, an old house overlooking the sea. It's been closed up for years—it's supposed
to be haunted. I'd thought of going there."

"I know the place, the old Smugglers' House. But mightn't
your family look for you there?"

"I doubt they're so determined to find me that they'll
search every town on the coast. They'll think themselves well
rid of me . . . still, perhaps I should just take a room in a cheap
sailors' inn—someplace out of the way where they don't ask
questions."

"It's The Crow's Nest you want. No one there wishes to be
recognized."

"It sounds charming."

"It will be a new experience for you, milady. I'll meet you
there after I've seen to your passage. Do you want to take the
first ship out of port, wherever it's bound?"

Nyctasia hesitated. She was not accustomed to revealing
her plans to anyone, but she would have to trust Corson this
far. "Get me passage to Lhestreq, if you can. What are your
plans now?" she asked, turning the subject as she always did
when questioned about her own affairs.

Corson smiled. "The first thing I mean to do is get flaming
drunk at The Jugged Hare—the owner is an old friend of
mine. He's a darling man, big as a giant and handsome as they
come . . . with green eyes and a bushy black beard," she added
dreamily.

Nyctasia shrugged. "I prefer them clean-shaven, myself. I

like to be able to see their faces."

"Have you got a pretty face waiting in Lhestreq?"

"Inland from Lhestreq," Nyctasia admitted. "And very pretty indeed."

"What does he look like?"

"Well, he's very dark, all except for his eyes—sapphire blue eyes. And he has long, black hair. I like long hair," she teased.

Corson looked away, blushing.

"He's lean," Nyctasia continued, "no taller than most, but he has long, muscled legs . . . hollowed hips . . ."

"Mmm," said Corson appreciatively.

". . . and a fine prominent collarbone, all ridge and shadow —I've missed that collarbone."

"I can see why you didn't marry your cousin."

"There was no lack of reasons for refusing him."

"Do you mean to marry the one with the collarbone?"

Nyctasia shook her head. Among families of the highest nobility, marriage was purely a matter of political convenience—a way of confirming an alliance or establishing a dynasty. As far as Nyctasia was concerned, love was a matter quite unrelated to wedlock. "I see no reason for it. Do you mean to marry that bearded giant of yours?"

"I don't know—maybe someday. But I couldn't spend all my life in Chiastelm. I get restless. And I'm dangerous when I'm bored," she said, only half joking.

Nyctasia smiled. "Perhaps you'll grow bored with wandering, someday."

"That's what Steifann says. He had his fill of traveling when he was a boy on the boats, and now he has his own place he means to stick to it." Corson gazed absently into the distance. "He's been right about most things," she admitted.

They rode in silence for a time, each lost in her own thoughts.

* * *

When they were within a few miles of the city gates, Nyctasia turned the horses loose and drove them off. "I want to enter the city on foot. A poor student doesn't own horses like these."

Before she'd learned of their strange pedigree, Corson had

hoped to have the fine horses in fee, but now she watched them trot off without much regret. "But won't they come back to you again?"

"Not if I send them away myself. They'll return to my stables, and I pity anyone who tries to stop them." She looked down at her stained and bedraggled attire. "I suppose I look as though I've been walking for days," she said, scuffing her boots in the dust of the road. "I certainly feel like it." She cut herself a stout branch for a staff and blunted one end against a rock to make it look travel-worn.

Corson watched her with distrust and a certain grudging admiration. "Lady, you have the cunning of a sneak-thief."

"And that's another thing—take care you don't call me 'Lady' once we're in the city. Only one person in all Chiastelm knows who I am."

"The moneychanger."

"Well, no, in point of fact, I—"

"No?!" shouted Corson. She advanced on Nyctasia menacingly. "Was anything you told me the truth? What about my money? What about your rutting honor?"

"Now Corson, don't be hasty—listen to me," said Nyctasia quickly. "I can explain!"

9

NYCTASIA WAS WELL-KNOWN at the humble establishment of
Vroehin the Moneychanger. But she was known as an imperti-
nent messenger-boy from the household of the Lord Heirond,
an elderly, bedridden nobleman who had never laid eyes on
her. He would have been most surprised to learn that large
sums had been deposited in his name with one of the lesser-
known banking houses on lower Market Street.

As they approached the entrance, Nyctasia held her
shoulders straighter and put a jaunty swagger into her walk.
Her grey eyes were bright with amusement as she surveyed
the shop. It hadn't changed. Thin, middle-aged Vroehin still
bent over his table of measuring rods and scales, his young
daughter perched on her tall stool behind the counter, ready to
record the day's transactions.

Nyctasia flashed them her cockiest grin. "Good luck to this
house!" she said in a voice both louder and mellower than
usual.

"Well, well, Master Rastwin—we've not seen you here in
some time. Mellis has been pining away for you."

"Father!" chirped the girl, "I have not!"

"Why not?" Nyctasia demanded, drifting in the direction of
the comely young bookkeeper. "Still hard-hearted as ever, and
me dreaming of you by night and day?"

Vroehin snagged her by the belt and pulled her back.
"Let's hear your business, youngster."

"My lord's instructions are, you're to pay this ruffian what
she asks. Asye knows what she's done to earn it. Cut some-

46

one's throat, I shouldn't wonder." She winked at Mellis. "Nice company for a gentle lad like me!"

Corson gestured threateningly at her. "Keep a civil tongue in your head, boy, if you value that pretty face of yours!" She joined Vroehin at the counting table.

Nyctasia backed away, laughing insolently, and leaned over Mellis's counter. "Mellis wouldn't let you touch me—she'd scratch your eyes out first, wouldn't you, Song of my Heart?"

"Someone ought to give you a good beating, you pest. Maybe that would teach you some manners." She surveyed Nyctasia critically. "And how did you lose your earrings? Gambling again?"

"Cards," said Nyctasia promptly, "are my only weakness, aside from beautiful, cruel, passionate girls. But next time I'll win, and buy you a gold locket, honeycomb." She hoisted herself lightly up on the counter and tugged at one of Mellis's yellow braids.

The girl tossed her head. "Oh, I've heard about you," she lied. "It's not just for your insolence that Lord Heirond keeps you!"

"Well, and what's the harm to you if I warm an old man's bed for him now and then, you selfish wench? There's plenty of me left for you." She snatched the girl's hand and kissed it. Mellis swatted her.

"Father!"

Without looking up from his counting, Vroehin snapped, "Get off of there!"

"Just as you say," said Nyctasia, and leaped down on Mellis's side of the counter.

Corson heard scuffling and Mellis giggling, "Behave!" She was torn between watching Nyctasia's performance and watching the moneychanger count out her pay. The money won.

"Quite the young rake," she said, after Vroehin had collared Nyctasia and shown them both the door. They walked up Market Street. "What if that girl decides to marry you?"

Nyctasia smiled. "Oh, Mellis may flirt with a good-looking rascal, but she's not fool enough to marry one. She's engaged to a steady, hardworking apprentice at one of the best financial houses." Her voice was warm with affection and respect. "That one's sharp as a spur! Only fourteen, and she's been keeping Vroehin's accounts for two years."

Corson walked on in moody silence. "Do you use magic to make them think you a boy?" she said at last.

"No need for that. I don't make them think it, I let them think it. People see what they expect." She threw back her head with a sudden boyish grin that made Corson want to cuff her. When she looked at Nyctasia now she could see the mocking youth who had been there all the time. She spat.

"No wonder everyone in Rhostshyl wants you dead!"

"Don't be jealous, my sweeting," Nyctasia said smugly, "why, the girl means nothing to me!" She dodged out of Corson's reach, laughing, then suddenly resumed her usual stance and manner. They had come to the market square. "This is where we part company. You'll get the rest of your money tonight."

Corson stared at her, exasperated. This was like snatching at a gadfly. "I'm going this way," she growled, pointing to the busy thoroughfare. "I'll meet you tonight at The Crow's Nest and take you to the docks. All I want is to see the last of you."

Nyctasia bowed. "Until tonight, then. Don't keep me waiting—I'll be counting the moments till we meet!"

10

NYCTASIA TOOK A roundabout route to the home of Maegor
the Herbalist, circling back erratically through the tangled
sidestreets till she was satisfied that no one followed. When
she entered the apothecary's shop, Maegor merely glanced up
and waved her into the back room without a word. Then,
when her customer had gone, she locked the front door and
joined Nyctasia among the shelves of jars and mortars.

Maegor was a handsome, hill-bred woman, serene and
thoughtful, and not much given to talk. She was one of the
few people Nyctasia trusted.

"I love the way it smells in here, Maeg. It makes me feel
calm, and that's not easily done."

Nyctasia had already fetched her belongings from their
hiding place beneath a loose flagstone. She slid a chest back
over the cache and perched on top of it.

The herbalist embraced her. "'Tasia, I thought you'd been
killed! There were all sorts of rumors—"

"Good," said Nyctasia. "Don't let it be known that I'm
alive. So many people would be disappointed." She took some
dried fruit from a bin and nibbled at it.

"You mean to leave for good, then. Is there no other way?"

"Maeg, my life isn't worth a copper in Rhostshyl! It's not
only that my Great-Uncle Brethald tried to poison me—"

"Is he the one who died recently?"

Nyctasia did not seem to hear the question. "But," she
continued, "the Teiryns are howling for my blood, the stupid
swine, and when I engaged a mercenary escort, I found she'd

already been hired to kill me. By both Edonaris and Teiryn."

"Nyctasia! You're making that up."

"You know me better than that, Maeg. As if I'd invent a story so improbable!"

Maegor sighed. "Yes, your lies are always more convincing than the truth. And what became of this mercenary?"

"Oh, I kept her, of course. She seemed to consider it a professional triumph to cheat two employers at once." Nyctasia laughed. "I like her."

"You would. A hired killer! Was there no one you could trust among your own guard?"

"I'd be long dead if there weren't. But my people are Rhostshylid—how could I ask them to go into exile with me?" She began to pace about the narrow storeroom. "If they ever returned to the city after that they'd be condemned as traitors." Nyctasia kept her doubts to herself. Her own people would have been a constant reminder to her of the duties she was abandoning, the responsibilities of her rank. Better to travel with someone like Corson, whose lack of respect for her was rather a relief. "At least a hired killer can be bribed," she remarked to Maegor. "It's the sort with a personal grievance that's really dangerous."

"'Tasia, I think I'd rather not hear these things." She took Nyctasia's hand, which was sticky from the dried fruit. "Come wash up, and I'll give you a meal. You look scruffy as a vagabond student."

"I can't stay that long, Maeg," Nyctasia said regretfully. There was nothing she would have preferred to a bath. "I'm supposed to look like a vagabond student, anyway. Maybe I should put a few more patches on this cloak."

Maegor shook her head. "I'll fetch you some scraps of cloth."

Nyctasia looked through the valuables she'd left with Maegor, picked out those she wanted, and replaced the rest under the floorstone.

Maegor returned with the cloth. "What are you doing?"

"The rest of this is yours. I can't take all of it with me."

"I'll keep it for you then. You may need it. You'll be back one day."

"I'd be crazy to come back!"

"You are crazy. All the Edonaris are crazy."

Nyctasia smiled sadly. "Maeg—"

"If I need the money I'll use it, 'Tasia," Maegor said firmly. She held out needle and thread.

Nyctasia could sew neatly enough for a noblewoman who rarely did such things for herself. But now she added the extra patches with a student's stitches, hasty-looking and irregular.

"How do I look?"

"Disreputable."

"I'm ready, then." She took out a letter sealed with plain, unstamped wax. It was an order for the release of certain prisoners, Rhavor's young servant among them. "Will you see that this is sent, next week when I'm well away from here? Give it to a traveler, someone who doesn't know you, and if you're asked—"

"I know, my dear. Say a stranger gave it me."

"Yes, isn't it exhausting? This sort of thing leaves me no time for my studies. Imagine what it will mean to be someplace safe, where I needn't constantly scheme to stay alive."

Maegor appreciated the vagueness of Nyctasia's "someplace." Nyctasia never gave herself away. The *vahn* alone knew what this devious existence was making of her. The herbalist feared for her friend's life, but she feared more for her spirit.

"Lie if you think best, 'Tasia, but I'd like to know—are you going to join Erystalben?"

Nyctasia hesitated over her answer, which would of course be something ambiguous like "If I can," or "I'd like to."

"Yes, I am," she said, breaking into a smile.

"I'm glad." She walked Nyctasia to the door. "I'll miss you, but you're right to go. You've learned the ways of your enemies too well, 'Tasia. You might forget that there are other ways."

Nyctasia shrugged. "People learn what they must, to survive."

"I wonder. If you must destroy yourself to defend yourself, have you truly survived? Be careful, 'Tasia."

For answer, Nyctasia only turned to Maegor and hugged her as hard as she could. For once she had nothing to say. She never told people she loved them.

11

CORSON PUSHED HER way into the crowds thronging the busy marketplace. "Hlann take her," she muttered, "misbegotten witch!"

She wandered through the square, fingering the heavy pouch at her side, and the weight of the coins soon restored her good temper. On every side were merchants' stalls piled high with all manner of goods. Corson admired velvets and rich brocades, brass lanterns and stout carved chests. She passed a potter at his wheel, shaping a graceful bowl.

Further on, a woman had set up a brazier and was cooking meat and vegetables spitted on wooden sticks. Fat dripped down onto the coals, and the smoke was fragrant with thyme and rosemary. Corson bought a skewer and walked along eating it. Across the way, a gypsy child with a draggled peacock on a leash was offering the feathers to passersby, two for a silver penny.

She would ordinarily have lingered in the marketplace, but today Corson was eager to get to The Jugged Hare. And there was still the matter of Lady Nyctasia's passage out of Chiastelm to take care of. She threw the stick to the ground and wiped her mouth on her sleeve. Steifann might know of a trustworthy cargo-runner—he'd once worked on the docks, and many sailors frequented his tavern. She should be able to find out what she wanted to know without mentioning Lady Nyctasia.

But as she set off in the direction of The Jugged Hare, her

attention was drawn by the faint sound of bells and a heady fragrance of incense, both wafting from a small striped tent in a far corner of the marketplace. As she came nearer, she could see wind-chimes and silver bells hanging from the awning, with prisms and pendants of crystal strung among them.

Corson hesitated. Like most soldiers, she was a reckless spendthrift, and the more outlandish and costly the merchandise, the more it appealed to her. She was itching to spend some of her hard-won gold, but if she went right to The Jugged Hare, Steifann would insist that she put most of it aside for safekeeping. That decided her.

She had to stoop to pass the curtained entranceway, but inside the tent there was room enough to stand straight. The ground was covered with a scarlet carpet, strewn with a tantalizing array of candlesticks and vases, bright scarves, bowls of beaten brass and figurines of jade. Strings of glass beads spilled from an open chest. Corson stepped through the haze of perfumed smoke, lit only by hanging oil-lamps, and examined in turn a damask sash and an ivory-handled knife. Kneeling by the chest, she fingered pearl necklaces and brooches of nacre in silver filigree.

The proprietor, who had paid no attention to her at first, now came up and made her a deep bow.

"Good day to you, Star of Warriors. Which of my humble trinkets has pleased you?"

Corson shrugged disdainfully. "These are pretty toys, but I've no use for such things."

He spread his hands in resignation. "Ah, no doubt your many lovers have showered you with treasures. It is no wonder you are indifferent to my poor baubles. And, in truth, a woman as fair as yourself has no need of further adornment. But if you permit me, I will show you the one thing that such beauty requires." He invited Corson to sit on a tasselled cushion while he fetched a coffer of rosewood from a corner of the tent. From this he drew forth something swathed in cream-colored silk, and Corson watched in amusement as he ceremoniously unwound the wrappings.

"Perfection is not to be enhanced, but enjoyed," he said, and held up before her an ornate silver handmirror.

She took it from the merchant carefully, almost reverently, and studied the delicate molding of the frame and the intricate chased patterns on the back and handle. Her fascination was plain to see.

"It is a good piece," the man said casually. "You understand that I do not show it to you to sell, but only because I know that you will appreciate the artistry of the work. I would not insult you by mentioning money."

"A gold crescent for it," said Corson.

He laughed. "My dear child, those engravings were three years in the making. It is a gift at five."

"Sir, I am only a poor soldier—but I do admire genius. A gold crescent and six in silver."

"Poverty is a widespread disease. I myself," he sighed, "have devoted my life to beauty. It is not a lucrative profession. Four gold crescents."

Corson got up to leave, shaking her head. "It grieves me, but. . . ." She held out her hands to demonstrate their emptiness.

"I defame the artist who made this his life's work," he murmured, as if to himself. "Three gold crescents."

"Done," said Corson, and they both smiled. After a further exchange of compliments, she took her leave and stepped out into the sunlight, blinking. "What an old thief!" she thought. "Star of Warriors!"

She had not gone far before she took the mirror from her pack and lovingly examined it again, grinning in anticipation of the scolding she'd get from Steifann for her extravagance.

In Corson's rootless existence, Steifann was the one steadying influence. The Jugged Hare was her only home, and Steifann and his people her family. He kept her money and belongings for her, worried about her, argued with her, and had a lecherous nature that equaled her own. Though she never stayed in one place for long, Corson came back to the Hare whenever she could.

* * *

She'd first strayed into the tavern on a rainy night some years back, already half-drunk, and in a foul temper. Not only was she tired, wet and hungry, but she'd lost all her money gambling at The Pelican.

"Pelicans!" she muttered, and sat down at a table in a dark corner. "Vultures—all of them! They cheated me." She looked around the room miserably. It was late and the place was nearly empty. "And I'm lonely."

A serving-woman came over and asked if she wanted something to eat or drink. "Both," said Corson promptly. She took the woman's hand and kissed it. "What's your name, pretty one?" But the woman only gave her an arch smile and walked away, hips swaying.

"What's the difference?" Corson thought. "I can't pay for anything anyway."

She was served a cold supper of roast beef, cheese and a loaf of bread, which she tried to gulp down as quickly as possible, since she expected to be thrown out at any moment.

Then the serving-woman put a mug of ale before her, and held out her hand for payment. "A silver crescent, please."

Corson stuffed some meat into her mouth and shrugged. The woman waited.

"Go to The Pelican," Corson growled. "I left all my money there." She yawned and leaned her head on her hand.

"Steifann!" the woman called.

"Asye take them all," thought Corson. "I want to go to sleep."

Then a tall, broad-chested man with thick black hair and beard came out of the kitchen, wiping his hands on his pants. "What's the matter, Annin?"

The woman pointed to Corson.

"You, get out of here," he said, advancing on her threateningly. He had green eyes and fair skin.

Corson was in love.

She looked up at him with a ravishing smile. She rarely met anyone as tall as herself. "I like green eyes," she said.

Steifann jerked his head towards the door. "Up!"

Corson could have wept. She was still hungry, she had no place to sleep, she had no money, it was raining, and now a man she found overwhelmingly attractive was trying to throw her out into the street. "It's not fair," she mumbled. "Go away."

She watched him from the corner of her eye, and when he bent over to grab her arm she shoved the table into his stomach and sprang to her feet, leaving him doubled over and gasping.

When he'd recovered his breath, he leaned on the table and

told Corson in a tense, quiet voice precisely what manner of lice-ridden bitch he, Steifann, considered her to be. Then he vividly described how she might amuse herself after he had thrown her into the gutter where she belonged.

But Corson wasn't listening. When he came at her again, she backed away, laughing. "I think you're beautiful," she said, and hit him on the jaw. Steifann staggered against the table, lost his balance and fell, dragging Corson down with him. He rolled on top of her and tried to pound her head against the floor.

Corson didn't even try to fight him off. Instead, she wrapped her legs around his hips and pulled him closer, sliding her hands under his clothing. "Don't go," she protested, as he leaped up, gasping, his face red. Annin and the few remaining customers stood staring, while a cook and serving-boy watched from the kitchen doorway.

"Get her out of here!" Steifann shouted at them. "Call the watch if you have to, but get rid of her!" He strode into another room and slammed the door behind him.

Heartbroken, Corson got to her feet, gazing at the sturdy oak door. She towered over everyone in the room.

Annin and the cook looked at each other. "You heard him," said Annin. "Get her out of here."

"I'm the father of children! You get rid of her!"

"What's back there?" demanded Corson.

"That's Steifann's quarters!" the kitchen-boy said gleefully, before the others could stop him.

Corson made up her mind, crossed to the door and kicked it open. From within, they heard Steifann yell furiously, "You rutting cur, get out of here! I'll kill you!"

"No!" The door slammed again. "Don't be a fool!" Sounds of struggling and cursing ensued, followed by a crash of falling furniture.

"Stop that, you—"

"Why?"

". . . uhh. . . ." The room became very quiet.

"Maybe they've killed each other," Annin whispered.

"Do you want to go in and find out?"

"Not I." They shooed out the last customers and began gathering the dirty platters and righting the overturned table and chairs. Annin bolted the shutters. A scullion started sweeping the floor.

Suddenly, the silence was punctuated by a series of deep, staccato cries. The kitchen-boy giggled. "That's the way I want to die," he sang, snatching up the broom and dancing around with it.

"Put out the lamps, Trask!" Annin ordered. "You useless brat!"

12

THE SIGN AT Steifann's tavern showed a large, leering hare drunkenly embracing a jug of ale. Corson looked up at it fondly, remembering how the hare had seemed to wink at her the first time she'd seen it, inviting her to enter.

She went around to the back entrance, hoping to find everyone together in the kitchen. She'd been away longer than usual and her friends would fuss over her and scold her. Walden, the head cook, would complain that she was too thin, Annin would make her take a bath, and Trask would flirt with her—but then, Trask flirted with everyone. And Steifann would hug her so hard he'd lift her off the ground, all the while demanding to know where she'd been, what she'd been doing, and with whom she'd been doing it—but without really expecting any answers. Corson hurried through the courtyard to the kitchen.

Walden was scowling over a huge stewpot when Corson came up from behind and hugged him. "I'm starving," she said.

"Corson, you rutting idiot! What are you doing here? They'll find you!" he looked around anxiously. "Trask, get Steifann."

The serving-boy gave Corson a horrified look and rushed from the room.

Bewildered, she drew her sword and backed towards the door. "Who'll find me? Where are they, out front?"

"Not yet, but they're bound to come sooner or later—you're well-known around here."

"Asye's Blood, man! Who are you talking about?"

Steifann came in from the front room, bolting the door behind him. "What are you all gaping at? Corson's not here, everyone knows she's left town. Corson, put that sword away before you kill somebody." He pushed the hair back from his forehead distractedly. "We'd better go to my room," he said at last, "and make some plans." He led Corson out the back way.

"Get back to work," said the cook. "Nothing's happened here. Get that spit turning before the birds burn!"

Corson dropped onto the bed and slapped the space beside her. "Steifann, what is this all about?"

He sat down and put his arm around her. "You stupid ass, don't you know there's a price on your head? Two hundred crescents in gold for the capture of a tall, left-handed swordswoman called Corson. Or one hundred for killing her. There's a lot of people in this city who'd sell you for half that."

"But who offered the money? Who wants me that badly?"

"They say he's some great nobleman from Rhostshyl. And there are other rumors about him, Corson. . . ." Steifann hesitated. "I don't think he has an easy death planned for you."

Corson looked away. "Threats," she said carelessly. "Well, is there anything else I should know?"

"He's looking for someone else as well—a small, dark-haired woman. And there's five hundred crescents to be had for her. His servants have gone to every rat hole on the docks, and every ship in port." Steifann felt Corson's shoulders suddenly tense, and he looked at her sharply. "She's down there, isn't she?"

Corson didn't answer. Instead, she threw her arms around Steifann and kissed him hard, then stood up and shouldered her pack.

"Corson, don't be a fool! What are you going to do?"

"Run! Run like a hare from the hounds!" There was a knock at the door, and Corson's hand dropped to her sword hilt.

"Steifann, let me in," said a woman's voice impatiently. Corson laughed with relief and shot back the bolt to admit a short, stocky woman of forty with broad hips and an ample bosom. Annin had been head serving-woman at The Jugged Hare for years, and was firmly convinced that only her common sense and good judgment kept the tavern from ruin. The fact that Steifann was the owner did not prevent her from treating him as one of her underlings.

"Corson, my lamb, you oughtn't to be here, it's too dangerous. Have you no sense at all?" she scolded.

Corson bent down and kissed her. "I'm not here, I'm leaving. You take care of Steifann for me."

"You're not going anywhere till dark," Annin said firmly. "You'd be seen. How do you think you'd get out of the city?"

"I think she means to go straight to the docks and warn that woman," Steifann broke in.

"Rubbish," snapped Annin, and pushed Corson back onto the bed. "Sit down."

"I don't have time to argue, Annin, I—"

"Then don't. If you want to warn someone, you can send a message."

"That's right," said Steifann. "I know my way around the waterfront. When I was working on the wharves—"

"No. Not you," said Annin. "You're so rutting big, folk take note of you. I'll go myself, tonight. With a shawl over my head, no one will notice me."

Corson shook her head. "This is my affair, Annin. I know what I'm doing."

"You don't know your left hand from your right. Every informer on the docks is looking for you. You won't do yourself or anyone else any good by getting caught." Hands on hips, she fixed Corson with a fierce, protective glare. "You'll stay out of sight until we can get you safely away from here."

"Destiver's ship is in port," said Steifann. "If we take the wagon down to the wharf before dawn, maybe we can smuggle her aboard. There'll be plenty of carts unloading supplies and cargo."

"Who's Destiver?" Corson protested. "I'm not—"

"Good idea. I could arrange that now. Both of you wait here till I get back. Is that understood?"

Corson was silent.

"She's right, you know," said Steifann. "You can't go down there. You might as well walk into their arms."

"Where is she, Corson?" Annin demanded.

Corson got up and paced the room restlessly. She'd never involved her friends in this kind of thing before, but she knew that she had no choice. She couldn't protect Lady Nyctasia by walking into a trap. A feeling of helplessness swept over her, and to Corson it seemed, as always, a foretaste of death. She clenched her fists. "I don't like it."

"I know," said Steifann. "You'd rather get yourself and that other woman killed than admit you need help." He waited.

Corson looked at the floor. "She's at The Crow's Nest. I'm supposed to get her on a ship tonight."

Annin nodded. "I'll see about passage for both of you then. I can take her straight to the ship after dark, but meanwhile I'd better go talk to Destiver. And, Steifann," she added sternly, "don't let her out of here!"

Steifann raised Corson's head and kissed her. "Now what can I do to keep you here till Annin gets back?"

She put her arms around him and pulled him close. "I thought I'd be able to stay with you awhile," she sighed, leaning her head on his shoulder.

"I don't want you to go."

There was nothing more to say. He held her against him and stroked her back gently, then reached up to loosen her long braid. Corson tilted back her head and shook free the bronze cascade of her hair. His lips brushed along her throat, and he began to kiss her on the mouth and eyes. Corson pressed against him and slid her hand between his legs. She heard his breathing change and he held her even tighter.

"Corson . . ."

"Mmm . . . ?"

"Will you take off that rutting sword, or do you want to make a gelding of me?"

"Asye forbid!" laughed Corson, letting her sword belt slip to the floor, and pulling him down onto the bed.

13

No one looked up as Nyctasia entered The Crow's Nest, or offered to assist her in any way. She went up to a group of idlers gathered around the fire and slammed her stick down across a bench. "Ho, the house! Who keeps this vipers' den?"

A man and woman glanced askance at each other. The man shrugged. "What do you want?"

"What do I *want?*" echoed Nyctasia. "I want accommodations fit for a queen, of course. I want splendor, gaiety, and lordly fare. Spiced delicacies and ruby wine! That's what I want!"

Shouts of agreement arose from the other guests. This was the best entertainment they'd seen in some time.

"I could do with some of that myself!"

"Tell us more, woman!"

"I want decent lodgings," Nyctasia concluded, "but I'll settle for what you've got to offer."

This sally too was met with cheers. "Best lodgings this side of the gutter, right here!"

"If you happen to be a rat or a roach—"

"Most of you are," said the landlady, and spat into the fire. She stood and walked from the room, giving Nyctasia a hard look as she pushed past her. Nyctasia bowed elaborately, sweeping her shabby cloak out of the woman's way with an ironic flourish.

The group made room for her on the bench, hoping for more sport. "Do you have any money?" said the landlord. "We don't take clever speeches in payment."

"Oh, of course I'm carrying a fortune in gold and jewels," sneered Nyctasia. She tossed him a small silver coin. "Two nights," she said. She did not intend to stay for a single night, but it might be safer to mislead her listeners.

He examined the coin carefully, then nodded. "Any bed upstairs."

Nyctasia repressed a shudder. She was prepared to face danger and hardship, but nothing could reconcile her to the prospect of bed-lice. After joking with the other guests for a time, she made her way upstairs, claiming to be exhausted from a day's hard walking. She entered a large, slant-ceilinged room at the head of the stairs, noting that it had no other door and only one small window high on the far wall. There were several straw pallets in the room, but none that Nyctasia would have lain or even sat upon under any circumstances.

The other two rooms were similar, and she returned to the first, satisfied that she was alone. When she'd latched the door, she pulled a small leather bag from her shirt and took from it a pair of exquisite golden earrings. The lustrous red-gold shone softly, even in the dim light from the gable window. Edonaris heirlooms, they were part of the legacy from her late, unlamented Great-Uncle Brethald.

She smiled grimly. How it must have galled him to know that Nyctasia, a traitor to the name of Edonaris, would inherit the better part of his goods and properties. But he was childless, and inflexible tradition decreed that family property follow very specific lines of descent. It was no wonder he'd tried to ensure that Nyctasia would die before him.

Now she brooded over the beautiful golden earrings and thought how outraged he would have been to know that she considered giving family treasure to a base-born hireling. But Corson had surely earned them. She'd lost her own in Nyctasia's service, and it would be most appropriate to reward her with a new pair. Nyctasia herself wore only adornments of silver, to accentuate her grey eyes and fair complexion—gold was for honey-skinned Corson, or dark Erystalben.

But still Nyctasia's blood reproached her at the thought of thus estranging ancient Edonaris property. She weighed the jewelry in her hand thoughtfully. After all, had she not broken with her family? Why not celebrate her freedom with this gesture, if only to spite the memory of Great-Uncle Brethald?

Suddenly she leapt to her feet, hastily concealing the earrings. She could hear people climbing the stairs. The door was forced open before she could unlatch it, and three armed guards entered the room.

"We have orders not to harm you, my lady, unless you resist us. Will you surrender your weapons?"

Nyctasia at once resorted to the most convincing lie of all: she laughed. "My lady?" she cried, in seeming delight. "Oh, I like that! What would a lady be doing here, you imbeciles?" She minced up to the guard who had spoken, with the affected grandeur of an ill-bred student imitating a noblewoman. "Pray enter my ancestral halls," she invited. "Lady Maggot of Vermin Hall bids you welcome!"

The guards looked at one another, uncertain. "Maybe—" one of them began.

"Well?" demanded Nyctasia. "Here I am, arrest me! Her Ladyship of Quills and Patches!" She seemed to be having a wonderful time. "Ho, friends!" she shouted, for the benefit of the listeners downstairs, "you people didn't know you had a great lady in your midst, did you?"

But the laughter that answered her from the stairway was not that of her fellow lodgers. "Forgive me if I fail to applaud such a fine performance, cousin, but you see that I have the use of only one arm." The guards moved aside, and Lord Thierran ar'n Edonaris entered, smiling. His right arm was bound in a bandage and sling. "Be sure to gag her," he ordered. "She'll convince you that no one's here at all if she isn't silenced."

Nyctasia passed from desperation to despair. No one would come to her rescue now, for no one knew where to find her. She had been careful about that, as always. "But not careful enough," she thought bitterly. Only Corson had known where she was hiding. It must have amused her to be paid for changing sides once again. She must be very well pleased with herself.

14

STEIFANN ENTERED THE room quietly. Corson was still asleep, her hair spread loose on the pillows. He stood over her a moment and then placed his hand on her back. Without opening her eyes she grabbed his wrist and tried to pull him down on top of her.

"Stop that, woman," he said, sitting down beside her. "Get up." He slid his arms under her and lifted her up beside him. She leaned against him and mumbled something into his neck.

"What?"

"I'm cold."

He pulled her closer, cupping her breast in his hand. "Better?"

She nodded, then raised her head and kissed him.

"Will you listen to me? Some madman's got half the city hunting for you, and all you can think of is screwing."

"I'm thinking of food, too. I'm hungry."

"Corson—!"

"Yes. I'm listening."

"The *Windhover* leaves with the morning tide. Destiver's agreed to take the two of you."

"Oh," said Corson dispiritedly. "How much will it cost?"

Steifann cleared his throat and mentioned a sum. Corson gasped.

"If you don't have the money, Corson, I'll get it for you."

She was disgusted. The price would take most of what Nyctasia had paid her. All that hard-earned money gone—and for what? Curse Lady Nyctasia and her stinking family! "No, I can pay it. But what about the captain, Steifann, and the crew? Can they be trusted? What's to keep them from trying to collect the passage money and the reward too?"

"Don't worry, I know Destiver. She'll keep her word."

"She?" said Corson, her eyes narrowing suspiciously. "How well *do* you know her?"

"We're old friends," he grinned. "She'd do anything for me."

"Old friends? I know what that—"

They were interrupted by the arrival of Annin. "Corson, keep your voice down! And put your clothes on. There's no time to lose."

"What happened?" Corson demanded. "Did you find her?"

"I'm sorry, Corson, she's been taken. It's all over the docks."

Corson cursed softly. "What have you heard?" she said, pulling on her breeches.

"Wild rumors, mostly. This woman's a spy. A faithless wife. A foreign princess—or a prince, for that matter. They took her asleep, or, if you like, she fought like a demon and killed three guards." Annin shrugged. "But all the tales agree that they found her at The Crow's Nest and took her prisoner."

"Where did they go?"

"To Rhostshyl. Or to Liruvath. To a mansion in the center of town! Nobody knows. The question is, has she told them where *you* are? They might be here at any moment—we have to get you to the ship now! I'll fetch the cart. You lovebirds say your farewells, and don't be long about it."

As soon as she was gone, Corson belted on her sword. "They won't be after me, now that they've found her. They probably thought I could lead them to her. I'll be safe enough."

Steifann caught her in a bear hug and kissed her. "Why don't you take up some sort of honest work, you worthless wretch?"

Corson broke away reluctantly. "I'll be careful. Tell Annin not to worry."

He followed her to the door, trying to bar her way. "Corson, you can't go after that woman—you don't even know where she is! Or do you?"

"I might. If I'm wrong, I'll go to the ship without her."

"And if you're right?"

"I don't know," she admitted. "I'll probably go to the ship without her anyway. I'm not about to try anything foolish. I'll be back in a month or two, when this affair's forgotten." She kissed Steifann on the ear. "And if I find out you've been sleeping with this Destiver," she whispered, "when I come back, I'll kill you!"

Steifann cuffed her gently and let her go. "Send me word that you're safe," he said.

"I will—soon. Nothing will happen to me."

He watched her cross the courtyard. At the gate she turned and waved to him, then disappeared into the alleyway.

"I must be out of my mind," she thought. "I'm going to get myself killed!"

15

NYCTASIA HAD LET herself be taken prisoner without resisting. She was no match for three swords, and it better suited her dignity to surrender than to be seized by force. The one gesture of defiance left to her was to die in her own way, as befitted a devotee of the Indwelling Spirit.

She had known herself for dead the moment she'd heard Thierran's voice, and she wasted no time on flip replies or futile struggles. Even as he gave his orders, while the guards bound her wrists behind her, she had begun the spell that would end her own life. She had spoken the truth when she told Corson that it was harder to kill with spells than to heal, but magic is always easier to work upon one's self than upon another. And death itself may sometimes be a healing.

Nyctasia was hardly aware of where she was taken, or how. She did not notice the landlady's satisfied smirk, or the wondering stares of the others, as she was led out of The Crow's Nest. She heeded nothing but the voice of the *vahn* within her as it ceaselessly repeated her name. By the time she found herself alone with her captor, she had already achieved the trance known as the First Consolation—her name no longer held the slightest meaning for her.

Lord Thierran removed the gag from her mouth. "Well, 'Tasia, surely by now you've prepared some fabulous lie to persuade me to release you. Perhaps you can convince me that I died along with Mescrisdan."

His words came to Nyctasia from a vast distance. She considered them dispassionately, judged them unworthy of her attention, and forgot them at once. In a vague way, she knew that she was bound to a chair, that Thierran stood over her, but she no longer took an interest. She had begun to move towards the Second Consolation.

"Answer me, fool, while you have the chance. I have you and I can break you!"

Threats could not reach Nyctasia now, but the hard slap across her face did disturb her concentration for a moment. She looked up at Thierran without recognition and said the only thing that was in her mind, repeating it over in a flat, lifeless voice.

"Nyctasia ar'n Edonaris nyctasia arnedonaris nyctasiarnedonaris nycta . . ."

"Stop that!" Lord Thierran struck her again and again, infuriated by her indifference. It was precisely Nyctasia's indifference that had always enraged him. The blows stopped her chanting, but pain was only another Influence to hasten her towards death. Her eyes slowly closed, and Thierran could sense her calm conviction that he did not exist. For a moment it frightened him.

Like most of the aristocracy, Lord Thierran had been raised as a Vahnite in name only. He had never practiced the Influences, Balances, or Consolations, but he knew of them, and he knew that Nyctasia took the Discipline seriously. She rarely drank spirits. She never wept. There was no doubt in his mind that she was capable of dying from sheer willfulness.

"Nyctasia!" But it was useless to call her by name. He seized her shoulder, shook her. "Listen to me, curse you! I want you alive!"

Though shielded by the profound apathy of the Second Consolation, Nyctasia could not dismiss Thierran's promises as easily as she had his threats. The *vahn* would destroy itself only if the alternative were a less desirable death. If Thierran offered her life, she would have to listen.

"Do you hear me? You throw away your life to no purpose, witch! I have no mind to kill you!"

Without allowing a shadow of emotion to disturb the even surface of her impassivity, Nyctasia decided on her response. Eyes still closed, and with the same toneless, unnatural voice, she said, "You tried to kill me only days ago."

He smiled, triumphant. "No, cousin—I tried to capture you. If I had tried to kill you, you would be dead."

She considered this with detached impartiality. True, he could have killed her easily enough before Corson arrived, while Mescrisdan still pinioned her arms. But instead he'd toyed with her, taunted her. . . .

She would hear more. She allowed herself to look at him, but her face remained as expressionless as her voice. "What do you want of me, then?"

"Only two things, my dear 'Tasia. The first, of course, is your hand in marriage." He leaned toward her. "You know that the family thinks it my duty to take a hand in the management of your affairs. Scholars are a fanciful lot, after all, ill-suited for governing. When we're wed, you'll be able to devote yourself to your studies and leave such things to me."

Reluctantly, Nyctasia accepted the burden of hope. She would have to make an effort after all. "I see. You stand to inherit much more if I die as your wife."

He had wanted to make her look at him, but now he found her even gaze unnerving. He walked around behind her. "You might live longer as my wife than as my cousin, 'Tasia," he murmured, laying his hand lightly against her throat.

Nyctasia controlled her urge to pull away from his touch. Instead, she only stiffened her shoulders slightly, enough resistance to flatter his pride, but not enough to provoke him. If she pretended to consent too easily, he would not be fooled. "And how long do you think you'd live as my husband, Thierran?" she asked coldly.

He laughed. "Oh, 'Tasia, you'll have to hope that nothing happens to me. While you're under my protection the family will tolerate you, but if I should meet with an untimely death, my grieving widow would bear the blame, guilty or not. You wouldn't live through the funeral, my dear."

"That would be a pity," said Nyctasia, "I look ravishing in black."

She understood, now. She'd be forced to sign a marriage—alliance ceding control of her major estates to Thierran. Then, if she were not killed at once, she'd be held under guard in her own household. She would stay alive as long as it amused Thierran to keep her. "And what is the second thing you want?" she asked, without agreeing to the first.

His hand tightened on her shoulder. "The mercenary."

"What do you mean?"

"You know very well. Your hireling, who killed Mescris-dan and crippled my arm. It may never heal! Where is she?"

Nyctasia gave no sign of her astonishment. It was not Corson who had betrayed her, then.... This meant more to her than she would have expected.

"She could be anywhere on the coast by now," she said, with a slight shrug. "I sent her away long before I came to Chiastelm. She'd have told my whereabouts to anyone who paid the price. For that matter, how did *you* know where to find me?"

"I did not know, I suspected. When Shiastred left these parts he took ship from here. Others may have forgotten your upstart lover, but I was sure you'd follow after him. My people have combed the docks between here and Ochram, offering a large reward for you."

"Of course," thought Nyctasia wearily, "I betrayed myself." Aloud, she said, "I see I've underestimated you, cousin." He'd like that, the gloating snake. "I'll have to be more careful of that in the future, if I have a future."

"We'll discuss your future after you've told me where to find the mercenary."

"For *vahn's* sake, Thierran, forget about her! I told you I got rid of her days ago. She rode north on the border road and that was the last I saw of her. I don't know where she is now!"

"And will you pretend that you don't know who she is, either? Her name?"

"Well, she called herself Brendal, but—"

He chuckled. "'Tasia, I've known you all your life. Do you think I still believe your ridiculous lies? You called her Corson that night, have you forgotten? I mean to find her, and I'll have the truth from you one way or another, I promise you."

Nyctasia shook her head. "An Edonaris does not take revenge on an inferior. She acted on my orders, and only I am accountable, you know that. If you want vengeance so badly, you have me—and you can strangle me with only one hand!"

"I have other plans for you, but you will not shield my brother's killer from me, Nyctasia. You dare speak of the honor of an Edonaris, who have done everything in your power to disgrace our house!" He gripped Nyctasia's hair, pulling her head back. "This assassin is only part of the price you'll pay for your life, do you understand me?"

It was useless, Nyctasia realized. Nothing but Corson's blood would satisfy him. "No," she said simply. "I do not understand you. I never have."

"What does that mean?" he demanded, coming around to face her, furious. "You're in no position to—"

"It means that you can kill me any way you choose, Thierran, except one. I can still prevent you from boring me to death."

The way was still open to her, and she followed it easily now, meeting no resistance. She did not even have to close her eyes this time—past the Second Consolation, it made no difference.

Peace was within her reach at last, and life and death were reconciled. To cease to be part was to become one with the whole, to be not merely a life, but Life itself.

Nyctasia was content.

16

"I'M GOING TO get myself killed," Corson thought. "He probably has a dozen guards in there." From where she crouched behind a broken-down section of wall, Corson could see a light from one of the windows on the topmost story. The house was supposed to be deserted.

Corson knew she'd guessed right, and she hated herself for it. The last thing she wanted to do was to risk her life looking for Lady Nyctasia, but the Smugglers' House was the obvious place for Lord Thierran to bring her. It was Edonaris property, and it stood empty on an isolated stretch of cliffs.

She watched as two guards made a leisurely circuit of the house. "This is madness," she thought. "If I'm caught here that bastard will feed me to the seagulls. And Lady Nyctasia is probably dead already, there's nothing I can do. I'd better get away from here while I still can."

As the two sentries came around the corner into view again, Corson stood. "Ho, you there!" she shouted. "What are you doing here?" She scrambled over the wall and stepped out of the shadows. "I'm caretaker here and you'd best explain your presence before I summon the watch!"

The guards came up to her, swords drawn. "You'll have to speak with Lord Thierran," one of them said. "The house was opened at his orders."

Corson stepped back. "I've had no word of this. You're a couple of thieves and smugglers!" She continued to back away, drawing them further from the house.

"Don't be a fool. Come back here!"

Corson let him get within arm's reach, then swiftly brought up her sword. The sentry clutched at his stomach and crumpled to the ground. As the other ran to give the alarm, she bent and pulled the knife from its sheath on her boot, then sent it into the back of the fleeing figure.

Corson dragged the bodies out of sight behind the wall, then dashed for the house. The lighted window seemed to be miles above her, but she found a foothold in the uneven masonry and started to climb, cursing under her breath. She felt sick. She was sure that she would either be discovered, or fall and break her neck.

There were plenty of holds in the stonework, but heights made Corson dizzy, and she felt exposed and vulnerable, an easy target for anyone below. Sweat ran down her back and between her breasts. She knew better than to look down.

"Steifann is right," she thought with disgust. "Only a half-wit would do this sort of thing. With my looks, I could have been a royal courtesan. I could have had a palace. Silks. Satins. Ropes of pearls." She continued to climb.

Soon she was near enough to hear shouting from the open window. "I mean to find her, and I'll have the truth from you—"

Corson had to move up closer before she could hear Nyctasia's reply. "She acted on my orders, and only I am accountable. . . ."

Corson slowly climbed up alongside the window and edged over to peer around the casement. Lord Thierran stood with his back to her, hiding Nyctasia from view, and there was no one else in sight. Corson smiled and reached for her knife. It would be an easy throw.

"Simm! Danin! Where are you two?" someone shouted. The patrol had not reported on time, and some of the other guards had been sent to find their missing cohorts. "What are you doing out there, screwing in the bushes?"

For a moment, Corson froze. Then, shaking off her panic, she swarmed up the last few feet to the roof and threw herself flat behind a chimney. Soon she heard shouting and confusion, and she knew that the bodies had been discovered. Her one chance had been to get in unobserved, and now a whole company of guards was alerted to her presence.

When the noise had died away, Corson inched forward carefully to look over the edge of the roof. She could see no one in the yard, but they'd soon be searching the grounds for her, and her escape would be cut off completely. If she could reach the ground without being seen, she might be able to save herself, but it was too late to help Lady Nyctasia. By now Lord Thierran must have been warned. There was no time for duty or pride or sentiment.

But she had barely begun her descent when she heard footsteps approaching from the front of the house. Her last hope of escape was lost, and she felt a chill tingling between her shoulder blades where the arrow would strike.

The window was only a few feet to her left, and in a moment Corson had made up her mind and clambered over the sill. If she was going to die anyway, maybe she could at least kill Lord Thierran first.

But Lady Nyctasia was alone. There was blood on her mouth, and her shirt was torn at the shoulder. She gave no sign of seeing Corson, though her eyes were open and staring.

Corson hurried past her and flattened herself against the wall by the doorway. Lord Thierran was coming up the corridor, still shouting orders to his retainers. "I want guards at every entrance! Search the stables and the gatehouse!"

He strode across the room to the window and looked out anxiously over the grounds, watching for any movement.

Corson kicked the door shut. At the sound, Lord Thierran wheeled around and stared at her in disbelief. She was coming towards him, smiling, a dagger in her left hand.

17

Nʏᴄᴛᴀsɪᴀ ᴡᴀs ᴅɪsᴛᴜʀʙᴇᴅ by a faint impression that she had once, long ago, seen something that she should remember. She drifted in lazy indifference, beyond reach of thought or time. As easy to admit illusions as to dismiss them, now, for illusion and substance were the same. Calmly, incuriously, she enveloped the distant memory.

Two people crossed in front of her, going in opposite ways. Then they turned to face one another, and came together. One held out a hand, and the other bowed.

This dance did not interest Nyctasia. Memory was for the living. She withdrew, but the images continued to haunt her. Patiently, passively, she followed the vision again.

A woman passed before her and turned, then a man crossed to the other side, and turned. The woman went to him and reached for him. He bowed before her, fell at her feet.

Nyctasia became aware that she had witnessed a dance of death. Still she was unmoved. Life and death were one. Composed, remote, she waited.

Corson hurried past her, hid herself, drew her dagger. Thierran entered, crossing at once to the window. These shadows began to seem familiar to Nyctasia. She remembered Corson's smile when Thierran had turned and seen her waiting for him. Paralyzed with fear, he in turn had waited for her. She pushed him against the wall, forcing back his head, then slashed his throat with one smooth sweep of her blade. Her smile was as rapt and brilliant as a lover's.

* * *

Nyctasia knew a certain confusion. Had she dreamed these
things while she was among the living . . . or had she seen
them, unheeding, as she followed the ebb tide of her life? Was
not dream reality, and reality dream? Surely this vision could
not affect her now.

But other images took its place—Corson cutting her bonds
with a bloody dagger, rubbing her wrists, trying urgently to
tell her something. . . .

"He's dead, look! Nyctasia, wake up!"

She herself must be Nyctasia, then. But who was Nyctasia?
With the name came other memories, vague and confused.
Who was dead, herself or another?

It seemed to Nyctasia that she pondered endlessly over
events from the distant past, but as she moved from timeless-
ness to the present, Corson still stood over her, trying to rouse
her.

"Nyctasia, wake up, please wake up! If I have to carry
you—"

Her deliberations had lasted less than a moment, then. She
laughed. "Do you know," she said to Corson, with genuine
interest, "that's the first time you've ever called me by name?"

18

CORSON HAD ONLY hoped for a chance to take vengeance on Lord Thierran, and now that it was done she was almost surprised to find herself still alive. The house was still, and she realized that it might yet be possible to escape unseen, but precious time passed before she could rouse Nyctasia from her indifference.

Peering out the window, Corson saw lanterns moving below as guards searched the grounds for her. "We'll not get out this way."

Nyctasia looked down at Thierran's body curiously. "Ah," she said with satisfaction, "that really happened, then."

"Stop dreaming! They'll come to report to him soon— we've no time to waste. Do you understand?"

Nyctasia picked up her satchel and slipped the strap over her shoulder. "I'm ready."

Corson didn't believe her, but this was their only chance. She listened at the door, then opened it cautiously. "Is there another stairway?"

"The servants' stairs, through the room at the end of the hall." Taking a torch from the wall, Nyctasia led the way, moving as calmly as a sleepwalker.

It seemed to Corson that they had been descending the narrow staircase forever. "Where are we?" she demanded in a whisper.

"Almost down to the kitchen. But there's—"

Corson clutched her arm. "Quiet! Listen . . . they've found him." They raced down the remaining steps to the scullery, but Nyctasia continued down the dark stairway to the cellars.

"Come back! We'll be trapped down there!" Corson followed, cursing softly. She was going to die like a rat in a hole because of this witless witch! Already there were footsteps on the stairs behind her.

When she reached the bottom the door to the cellars stood open, but before she could enter, Nyctasia called from somewhere behind her. A faint light showed from the crawlspace beneath the stairs.

Corson crouched and squeezed herself into the angular opening, nearly falling headlong through a gaping hole in the floor. Nyctasia had already descended to an underground chamber and stood waiting at the foot of the ladder, her white face peering up anxiously in the torchlight.

Halfway down the steps, Corson let the flagstone drop gently back into place over her. She could hear the guards on the stairs just above her head.

"They can search the cellars for hours," Nyctasia whispered. "We're underneath them, so walk softly. There's a tunnel leading down to the cove."

Corson nodded. The smugglers' tunnel was a legend in Chiastelm, but its exact location had remained a mystery. They moved quietly away from the ladder, listening for footsteps overhead.

The chamber narrowed to a low passageway at the far end, and Corson had to stoop as she followed Nyctasia down the dark corridor. "I've heard stories of this place," she said, "but I thought they were all moonshine."

"So did I, till I bought the house. But then of course I searched for the tunnel. It wasn't hard to find."

"Then why haven't folk found it?"

"I suppose they did—if there was any treasure it was looted long ago. The City Governors secured the house after the owners were hanged."

"They say it's haunted," Corson remembered.

"Very likely it is," Nyctasia agreed absently. She paused, sniffing the air, and sneezed. A fresh salt scent cut through the dank air of the tunnel. "This is the place, you can smell the sea." She walked on for a few steps until a wide fissure appeared in the wall to their left. "We have to climb down there and jump."

Dropping to her knees, she thrust the torch out over the edge, and Corson looked down uneasily, trying to measure the distance.

"I can't see the ground."

"It's about ten feet, I think. But there are holds cut into the rock for part of the way down." She dropped the torch over the side and threw her bookbag after it.

"I hate heights," said Corson sadly. "Have you ever done this before?"

"Oh yes, it's simple." Nyctasia lay on her stomach and edged her legs out over the side, feeling for footholds. As she disappeared over the edge, Corson heard her remark, "Of course, we did it with ropes . . ." Sounds of scraping and kicking were followed by a loud thud and curses.

Nyctasia held up the torch, rubbing at her hip with the other hand. "Simple!" she said brightly, grinning up at Corson.

"I could have been a royal courtesan," grumbled Corson. "Get out of the way!" She landed on her feet by Nyctasia. They were in a large, natural cavern. "How far are we from the docks? Our ship leaves with the early tide."

"An hour's walk, I'd say. This way." They started off again, Nyctasia limping slightly. "Aren't you staying in Chiastelm, Corson?"

"I'd planned to, but your loving cousin offered a handsome reward for both of us. Now that he's been murdered, I'll be suspected."

Nyctasia considered. "It might be as well for you to stay away for a time, but I doubt that my family is much interested in you—they'll blame me for Thierran's death . . . and lay claim to my properties." She drew a breath. "The matter has gotten out of hand, you see. It's one thing for Mhairestri to have me killed secretly, but another to herald it abroad that the Edonaris are at each other's throats. As for you, you'll soon be forgotten if you stay shy of Rhostshyl and keep quiet about this affair."

"Oh well, I have friends in Lhestreq," Corson said resignedly. "I hope you have plenty of money, because we'll have to pay an outrageous sum for our passage."

"Don't worry, you know I can conjure gold from the elements."

Corson stopped in her tracks. "I want an answer," she said in deliberate, measured tones, "not a riddle, not a jibe! Can you pay or can't you?"

"You've no call to doubt—"

"Yes or no?"

Nyctasia was silent. Corson had earned her confidence, but trust had always been a luxury she could ill afford.

Corson faced her, arms folded. "Make an effort," she said drily. "You can answer a question if you try. Out with it!"

Nyctasia succumbed with a laugh. "Of course I can pay. Thierran would have killed me with pleasure and thrown my body off the cliff, but it would never have occurred to him to pick my pockets first."

"Of course. A gentleman."

"An Edonaris," said Nyctasia.

The ground grew uneven, sloping sharply downward, and Nyctasia found it harder to keep up the pace. She abandoned the dying torch and they stumbled on in the darkness until a dim light revealed the mouth of the cave ahead. Corson cleared a way through the barrier of roots and bracken, and helped Nyctasia scramble down the steep outcropping of rock to the beach. It still lacked some two hours to dawn.

But they had not gone far before Nyctasia stopped to lean against a pile of boulders. "Can we rest here awhile?"

"Not for long. We haven't much time."

"It isn't time I need," Nyctasia said obscurely. She pulled off her boots and walked to the ocean's edge, then knelt, motionless, head bowed, her hands in the water.

It was easier, much easier, than Nyctasia had expected, perhaps simply because she was exhausted. She had often undertaken fasts and vigils to achieve the same end, but now, almost effortlessly, she emptied herself of fear, of pain, of weariness. She allowed sensation and sentiment alike to flow out from her with the waves that caressed her and drew away again. She rested and was renewed.

Corson sat on a rock and watched her, worried. It was growing lighter. But Nyctasia knelt on the shore for only a moment, then rose and returned to her, ready to go on.

She was transfigured. Her grey eyes were silver in the sea's reflected light. She blazed with a vivid elation she could barely contain. Pointing out across the waves, she cried, *"There* is power! Why, the reason I bought the Smugglers' House in the first place—"

"I don't care! Just put these on and be quiet!" She shoved Nyctasia's boots at her. "We have to go faster."

To her relief, Nyctasia obeyed and fell into step beside her. But now she kept pace with Corson's long stride with seeming ease.

"I suppose that was more of your spell-healing?"

"No, that takes time, as I told you. This is a borrowed power. It's easy, you see, but therefore fleeting . . . Lightly won is lightly lost," she sang:

> "Lightly won is lightly lost
> Early flower, early frost.
> Wont to wanton, wont to weep,
> What is lent is not to keep,
> What is lent is not to keep!"

She laughed to herself. "I've never tried it before. It's called a spell of Perilous Threshold. It's really most interesting."

"I hate magicians," said Corson with feeling. "The only thing that keeps you on your feet is that you're just too crazy to know you can't go on."

"There's something in that," Nyctasia agreed.

But by the time they reached the clusters of fishermen's huts scattered along the shore outside of town, Nyctasia had begun to falter again. "No more of your witchery," Corson warned. "You'll draw attention to us." They had already attracted curious glances from the fisherfolk readying their nets in the half-light of early dawn.

"No fear. I'd not survive another attempt at that spell."

"We're not far from the docks. Lean on me."

"For anything one takes, one pays," Nyctasia sighed. She took Corson's arm and somehow kept walking. When they reached Merchants' Wharf, Corson was practically dragging her.

* * *

On board the *Windhover,* preparations for sailing were already underway, but some of the crew were still loading cargo from a wagon on the dock. A thin, middle-aged woman came up to Corson. "You're Steifann's friend?"

Corson nodded curtly. "Destiver?"

"Yes. You have the money?"

"I have it," said Nyctasia, before Corson could reply. "All of it."

"Follow me." Destiver motioned the sailors aside and led the way up the gangplank.

"You don't even know how much it is," Corson said to Nyctasia in an undertone.

"I imagine she'll tell me . . ."

Stopping at an open hatchway, the captain turned to Corson. "Get below and stay out of sight till we cast off. I'll settle with her now." Without a word, Corson climbed down the ladder into the cargo hold.

The only cabin below deck was a narrow, airless cubicle walled off from the rest of the hold. Corson had been in dozens of others like it, and every time she'd felt trapped and suffocated. She sat down on the bunk, which was too short for her to stretch out on, and mulled over her situation with resentment.

"Giving me orders!" she muttered. "Scrawny, swaggering, leather-faced bitch!"

Nyctasia entered the cabin and sat down, leaning against Corson. "I feel terrible," she remarked.

"Do you think she's good-looking?" Corson demanded.

"Who?"

"That filthy pirate!"

"Her?" Nyctasia yawned. "I don't know. I suppose so." She curled up on the end of the bunk and buried her face in her arms.

"She is not!"

"All right, she's hideous," Nyctasia mumbled. "Whatever you say." Her face was battered—a dark bruise had appeared over one cheekbone, and her lip was cut and swollen.

"Nyc . . . ?" said Corson. There was no reply. She sighed, and pulled Nyctasia to the center of the bunk, wrapping the thin blanket around her.

Nyctasia half-opened one eye. "Wha . . . ?"

"I decided to cut your throat after all."

"Oh." Nyctasia shifted to a more comfortable position, too worn even to object to the dirty pallet and coverings.

Corson sat on the floor, leaning back against the wall—she would not sleep until the ship was safely out of port. To pass the time, she took the precious handmirror from her pack and studied her features critically. She looked as tired and grimy as she felt. Her reflection grimaced back at her, and she laid aside the mirror to paw through her pack for something to eat.

"He's probably screwing Trask right now," she thought sourly.

19

"SHE'S PROBABLY LYING dead in a dungeon by now—I tell you, she's gone too far this time. She thinks she can treat this like one of her fool escapades, but these are powerful people! Rich nobles, whoever they are—they'll crush her!" Steifann groaned and reached for the pitcher on the table before him. It was nearly empty.

"No more of that," the cook said sternly, snatching it away. "You're drunk enough already." He turned back to the great mass of dough, kneading it rhythmically. The kitchen was already fragrant with the smell of baking loaves. "Corson knows what she's about. You fret over her every time like a broody hen and she always comes back whole and hearty."

"This is different, I tell you—"

"You always say that. I've no time for your babbling. And you should be on your way to market by now—it's almost light. The best'll be picked over before you get yourself there. If you come back with flyblown meat and rotten cabbage you'll cook it yourself!"

Steifann got to his feet with a grunt. "You'll see," he said thickly. "I've more to think of than cabbages!"

"That's right," said the cook, pushing him out the door, "onions. I want a bushelful. Don't forget."

In the courtyard, children of all ages were feeding the hens, gathering eggs, drawing water, and loading their arms with firewood for the kitchen hearth—all in the noisiest possible manner. They were mostly the offspring of the cook and his wife, who lived across the court, but they spent most of the day about the tavern, doing kitchen chores and running errands. Seeing Steifann harnessing the cart-horse, two of the smallest stopped throwing corn at each other and ran up to him shrieking demands to be taken along to market.

Steifann, who was feeling the effects of a sleepless night and too much ale, winced at their clamor and shooed them away. "Not today," he said absently, pushing the hair back from his face and frowning at nothing. "I shouldn't have let her go," he thought for the hundredth time. But he knew full well that the cook had spoken the truth.

When Corson heard the ladder creak under a heavy tread, she got silently to her feet and drew her sword, watching the door anxiously. She would be at a disadvantage in such close quarters, where she could barely stand upright. Surely it was only one of the crew. . . .

"Corson, are you in there?" Steifann pushed open the cabin door, laughing at her surprise. "Must you always greet me with that sword in your hand? It's not manners. If I'm not welcome, I'll take myself off."

Corson's eager embrace left no doubt as to his welcome. "What are you doing here? Is something wrong?"

"Oh, I just thought I'd come see you off . . . not that I was really worried. I knew you'd be all right."

"You're drunk!" laughed Corson. "You must have been up all night fretting, and there was nothing to it—it was a lark."

Steifann peered over her shoulder with bloodshot eyes. "Who's that?" he demanded. "Hlann Asye, Corson, you've only just come on board and you're already in bed with the cabin boy!" He crossed to the berth in two strides and glared down at the sleeping Nyctasia. "Oh. . . ." he said uneasily, turning away. "Never mind. I don't want to know." He stooped to avoid a low beam and leaned back against the wall, fumbling in his pouch. "You must need some money, Corson."

She pulled his hand away and pressed it to her cheek. "No, she paid our passage," she said, nodding towards Nyctasia. "That one has no end of money." She nestled against him and murmured, "but you don't want to hear about her." Steifann reached his arm around her waist and drew her close.

"You've not changed, I see, Steifann. Stinking drunk and

still hot as a buck in rut!" Destiver leaned in the doorway, one hand on her hip. "But you'd best get yourself ashore unless you plan to sail with us. The tide won't wait for you, lover."

Steifann stifled a yawn. "Well, if it isn't Black Destiver, the terror of the coast," he remarked amiably. "No thanks, Destiver. I've sailed with you before, and that was enough to make a landsman of me forever."

Corson was looking from one to the other with a frown. Steifann gave her a parting squeeze and she kissed him quickly.

Destiver stepped aside to let him through the doorway and slapped him on the backside as he passed her. "You were no rutting good as a sailor, that's what made a landsman of you."

"Corson, write and let me know where you are," he called over his shoulder, and disappeared up the hatchway with Destiver at his heels.

"I'll see you when I'm back in port," Corson heard her remark.

Corson spat after them and slammed the door shut. She felt the ship lurch and move out with the tide. Harboring bloody thoughts, she settled herself to sleep.

* * *

Steifann was late getting to market, but nothing could dispel his good humor that morning. He listened with considerable interest to the tales making the rounds of the marketplace. The talk was all of a monstrous demon that had murdered a nobleman and half his guard at the Smugglers' House the night before.

"Just vanished into the air, it did," gossiped a cheesemonger. "They say it's the Witch of Rhostshyl's doing."

Steifann nodded sagely. "It sounds like witchery to me," he agreed. He purchased a packet of gingerbread for the cook's children and loaded his provisions into the cart. He forgot the onions.

20

NYCTASIA SLEPT FOR a day and a night, and woke feeling worse than ever. Not only was she stiff and sore in every limb, but she felt violently ill as well. Spasms of acute nausea racked her, and each slow roll of the boat was an agony. She was sure that she'd been poisoned.

Corson strolled in, chewing on a piece of fresh-cooked fish. "Time enough that you woke up," she said. "I brought you some breakfast." She held out a tin plate with half a steaming fish on it.

Nyctasia gasped and rolled to the edge of the berth, her empty stomach contracting painfully, her throat constricted. "Take that away!" she choked.

"Hmm, seasick," Corson observed. She helpfully ate the rest of the fish.

Nyctasia lay back and shut her eyes. Her face was grey. "Is that all it is? But I'm dying!"

"That's how it feels. It takes a few days to pass, but you'll live."

Nyctasia's stomach began to heave again. She leaned over the side of the berth and groaned. "I don't *want* to live."

"Everyone says that. I'll get you some water. And a bucket."

"Days . . . ?" whispered Nyctasia faintly. She tried holding her breath but it didn't help.

"You should try to get some of this down," Corson suggested. "It's better to puke up water than your own insides."

"I know. Leave me alone."

Corson hesitated at the door. "Why can't you cure this the way you healed that wound?"

"Must you always ask questions?" said Nyctasia feverishly.

"Must you always tell lies? You said healing was simple."

"I've called on the *vahn* for so much already, Corson—to do it again so soon would violate the Balance . . . between the Dwelling and the Indwelling. . . ."

The ship struck rougher water and Corson could see the sweat break out on Nyctasia's face. Between fits of retching, the sorceress gasped, "There's more than enough imbalance aboard this vessel!"

She was bedridden for the next three days and slept as much as she could. There was some relief when the *Windhover* docked at coastal towns to take on or deliver cargo. While they rode at anchor, the rolling of the ship was easier to bear, but the time between ports seemed endless to her.

Corson slept on deck, only coming in now and again to see that Nyctasia drank a mouthful of water, and to complain about her own lot.

"You're just as well off without the swill they eat on this floating dung heap," she grumbled, sitting on the edge of the narrow berth and crowding Nyctasia. "If not for you, I could be feasting at the Hare right now. Steifann has the best cook on the coast."

"Will you please talk about something else, if you must talk?"

"There's nothing else *to* talk about. I've never been so rutting bored."

"Pity," said Nyctasia drowsily. "Let me sleep."

Corson wanted company—she missed Steifann. Nyctasia was an unsympathetic listener, and the crew regarded her with obvious suspicion. They were a close-mouthed lot who rebuffed her friendly advances, and she was certainly not willing to approach the captain. She chafed at the idleness and confinement she was forced to endure aboard ship—fishing was a poor pastime, and it was not yet safe for her to go ashore when they made port.

In desperation, Corson pulled over Nyctasia's satchel of books and opened one at random. Dead languages! Why couldn't Nyctasia have something that a person could read? The first passage that was intelligible to her seemed to be a recipe—but for what? What was bloodroot?

Corson hastily turned the page. She leafed through ballads, riddles, and puzzling verses that looked suspiciously like incantations. The rest of the book was blank. She chose another volume and began laboriously to spell out a long poem about a warrior's encounter with a seductive demon. This was much more to her taste.

Before long, Nyctasia turned over and groaned fitfully.

"Are you awake?" Corson asked.

"Unfortunately."

"What does *lirihran* mean?"

"It's an old word for 'twilight,'" Nyctasia answered dreamily. "But it means 'half-darkness,' you see, not 'half-light'. . . . It's only found in poetry nowadays." She suddenly sat upright, wide awake. "What are you doing? Leave that alone!"

"Why? I'm not reading your foul spells."

"Well, what are you reading?"

"I'm cursed if I know—it's about a demon, and it's nothing I'd have thought a *lady* would write."

"Oh, that," said Nyctasia, relieved. "I only translated it. That poem was written centuries ago."

"Really? Folk haven't changed much, then."

"Yes, that's the lesson of it. Perhaps I'll make a scholar of you yet."

Corson snorted. "I could teach you a few things—this chart's all wrong." She turned to a map of the southern constellations. "Everyone knows you can only see the Wolf in winter, and the Chalice should be further over here. If you tried to travel by this, you'd never know where you were."

"It's hard to make accurate charts from old books and hearsay. Show me the right positions," Nyctasia said eagerly.

"Surely," said Corson, stretching. "As soon as I've finished this story."

Nyctasia hadn't the strength for an argument. "Please yourself, that's harmless enough. But be careful how you meddle with my books, Corson. Words can be dangerous."

"What does *wisranupre* mean?"

"Give me that," laughed Nyctasia, "I'll read it to you." She found that she was feeling much better.

* * *

The *Windhover* was a small, single-masted merchantman with a crew of only six, including the captain. It was built for coastal trading but, as Corson soon discovered, the ship was more than a simple cargo-runner.

One night she awoke with the moon still high overhead. Some change that she could not immediately recognize had disturbed her sleep, and after a puzzled moment she realized that the *Windhover* was no longer moving—they must have dropped anchor. She soon heard the ship's boat being lowered and the crew moving about, talking in low tones.

Surely they weren't putting into port in the middle of the night? Curious, Corson stood and looked over the rail towards land, but she could see only an occasional flash of light on the beach. The boat was making silently for shore, the oars dipping without a splash.

Corson smiled complacently. Of course, a pack of smugglers! That's why the crew was so wary of strangers.

"What are you doing here?" Destiver demanded in a harsh whisper. "Get below where you belong and stop your spying!"

Corson rounded on her angrily, keeping her voice low with an effort. "Don't try me, you stinking water rat! Save your bullying for your crew! What's it to me if you cheat the trade laws?"

"Listen," hissed Destiver, "Steifann's vouched for you, but there's a fat price on your head—remember that, and forget what you've seen tonight."

"And I remember that they still have gibbets for smugglers in the Maritime cities."

"Then we understand each other," said Destiver. "But while you're on my ship you'll do as you're told."

Before Corson could reply, one of the sailors came over to fetch Destiver, who went off muttering imprecations against Steifann for involving her in this affair.

For once, Corson agreed with her.

21

NYCTASIA WAS DISAPPOINTED to learn that the *Windhover* never sailed out of sight of land. She had never been on a ship before, and once she'd recovered from her seasickness she was eager to learn all the workings of the vessel. She drew diagrams of the rigging in her commonplace book, inquiring the name and purpose of every part of the ship.

Corson was far too familiar with ships to share Nyctasia's enthusiasm, and she was more bored than ever now that Nyctasia was taken up with this new-found interest. The sight of Destiver was a constant goad to her temper, and the crew continued to shun her, taking their lead from the captain. She took to spending more time in the cabin, brooding and trying to puzzle out Nyctasia's books.

For a time, an illustrated herbal took her fancy, with its detailed drawings of leaves and brightly inked paintings of flower petals. She read: "The leaf of the Wolfhead Yarrow, when seethed in water or wine yields a tisane which may be taken against the catarrh, and when crushed in a mortar is most profitably employed in the preparation of a poultice for staunching of blood and the other humours of the body, for it possesses certain beneficial properties which make the flesh to draw together in such manner as may aid in the closing of wounds and the healing of purulence and suchlike maladies."

Corson yawned. She passed over the lengthy instructions for the preparation of the poultice, and turned to the next picture, which showed a thick-stemmed plant with large, dark purple blossoms. Here, as elsewhere in the book, a dry, faded cutting was pressed between the pages. This was Royal Swinebane, Corson learned, and its juice was so deadly that even its touch was dangerous. When it was set afire it gave off evil fumes that burned the eye and choked the throat. It was not safe even to smell the thing.

"Poisonous little witch!" Corson muttered. She closed the herbal, being careful not to touch the flattened Swinebane, and took up the last of the books, which was so small it fit in the palm of her hand. It was closely written in a minute script that Corson read with difficulty in the dim light of the cabin. But, as she began to decipher the text, she found to her dismay that it was a long, ponderous treatise of Vahnite philosophy, even more dull than Wolfhead Yarrow. Corson paged through chapter after incomprehensible chapter of Influences, Reflections, and Balances until she came at last to something that looked like poetry. Here, a note in Nyctasia's handwriting read, "Debased Version of the Fourth Reflection:"

> See in this enchanted mirror
> All things from afar draw nearer
> Till yond is nigh, and all is here
> For nothing is lost, as shall appear.
>
> Pierce if you please the shining's seeming
> Wake if you will the sleeper's dreaming
> Learn of lover, reck of foe,
> Find thy friend, thy rival know.
>
> Lift, if you like, the veil of distance
> Dare to deny its false Resistance
> Set at nought a thousand paces
> Recall thy steps, erase thy traces.

Corson read the verse again, then the brief precepts that followed. The spell made no sense, but it seemed simple enough to do—all that was needed was a mirror. "Learn of lover?" she repeated. It would be underhanded of her to spy on Steifann, of course, but no one would be the wiser, and no harm done.

Nyctasia had warned her to leave the books alone, and she herself distrusted magic, but the temptation was a powerful one for someone as jealous as Corson. She looked around guiltily, undecided, then quietly shut the door of the cabin. Fetching the mirror from her pack, she unwrapped it slowly, half hoping that Nyctasia would return and catch her out.

The cabin seemed to grow closer and smaller than ever as she knelt beside the book, clutching the mirror in one clammy hand. Her own voice sounded strange to her while she recited the words of the spell, and the mirror felt suddenly heavier. She glanced down at it, then remembered that she was not to look at it yet, and turned away. Had she seen something move in the glass just then? Corson resolutely shut her eyes, whispering Steifann's name, then waited for the space of twelve heartbeats. It was time—but Corson still hesitated, seized with nameless forebodings. Then, steeling herself, she opened her eyes wide and stared into the mirror.

22

NYCTASIA'S CURIOSITY ABOUT the *Windhover* only served to put the crew on their guard against her. It generally boded no good for them when someone took such an interest in their doings, and Destiver was doubly suspicious of her passengers after her encounter with Corson. When she found Nyctasia seated by the open hatchway making notations in her commonplace book, she was certain that the game was up.

"Give me that!" She snatched the book away, ignoring Nyctasia's protests. "What are you writing?"

Nyctasia pointed. "A description of those ropes securing the mast, all supporting each other. I find the balance of forces most interesting." She held out her hand for the book, but Destiver paid no heed. "See here," Nyctasia said coldly, "it merely says that two ropes attach to each side, and one each to the front and back."

Destiver could not read and she would probably have doubted the truth of this, had the drawings not confirmed Nyctasia's words. "Front and back!" she snorted. "The stays run fore and aft, and the shrouds run athwartships." She threw the book down beside Nyctasia, who seized it and immediately began writing again.

"Wait a bit!" she called after Destiver. "Which did you say were the shrouds?"

Destiver lost all patience. "Get out of my sight," she yelled. "Get below and stay out from underfoot or I'll have you keelhauled!"

Nyctasia was wise enough to obey, despite her vexation.

95

How dare a common sailor address an Edonaris in that manner! In Rhostshyl she'd have been pilloried and flogged for such insolence. "Peace, peace!" Nyctasia counseled herself. There were sure to be many more such indignities before her journey's end.

But these thoughts were driven from her mind at once when she pushed open the cabin door and saw Corson kneeling over the book of spells, staring into the silver mirror. "Corson!" she gasped. "What have you done?"

"Not a rutting thing!" shouted Corson. "I did just as it says, and here I am looking at my own face! I could do that without this crazy nonsense of yours."

Nyctasia picked up the book and looked at the spell with horror. *"Vahn* help us!" she whispered, sinking onto the bunk. "Corson, you fool—! Be thankful you didn't understand it. That's all that saved you."

"Saved me? From what?"

"From getting what you wanted! You might succeed in working that spell if you could read its meaning, but there'd still be the price to pay. All power has its price."

Corson had not considered this. "Like the spell you did on the way to the docks?"

"In a way. It's always dangerous to draw upon a power you don't possess. But if I use a spell of Reflection, I know what will be demanded of me in return, to restore Balance. When it's done blindly, without the proper preparation, it's like a weapon in the hands of a child. More is lost than gained."

"But I did as the book said. I followed it to the letter."

"I don't mean that absurd ritual," Nyctasia said impatiently. "All that's mere superstition to deceive the ignorant. Even the words of the spell are only the outward sign of the Principles of Power—power that could destroy you! To learn to wield that power takes years of discipline and study. *That's* the preparation I speak of. If that is lacking in you, the magic will exact its own sacrifice."

Corson was trying to find a way through the maze of Nyctasia's explanation. "Well, what would be taken from me?"

"There's no saying—I can only tell you what's happened to others." She opened the book of spells, turned over a few leaves, and began to read. "It is said that those who've seen their loved ones in the glass have never seen them again in life."

Corson paled.

"There is a tale," Nyctasia continued, "of a poor student who desired to learn whether he would marry the one he loved. Commanding a Reflection of the future, he saw the maiden lying upon her bier, at which sight he was so stricken with grief that he straightway took his own life. When tidings of this reached his lady, she did in truth perish of sorrow, and thus did the vision of the student come to pass.

"Others have been shown more than they could bear to see, and have lost their reason in consequence. There have been those who tore out their own eyes to escape from the sight—"

Corson had heard enough. "Very well, suppose *you* did it, what then?"

Nyctasia shook her head. "It would be safer for me than for most, but one doesn't undertake any spell lightly. The Discipline lessens the danger but cannot abolish it. Only the veriest simpleton would squander such hard-won mastery without good cause."

Corson knew that Nyctasia wouldn't find her jealousy sufficient reason for using the spell. "Oh, no matter," she said, disappointed. "I don't care about it, I was only looking for some amusement."

"For *vahn's* sake, Corson, you can't toy with such things! Promise you'll not try this again, please!"

"All right, all right, I promise. But the boredom's more deadly than those wretched spells anyway." She kicked fretfully at the side of the bunk. "What do *you* find to do all day on this rat-ridden scow?"

"Well, I was trying to learn something about the ship, but the captain ordered me to stop asking questions and stay below. What a surly-tempered creature she is."

Corson laughed. "You call me a fool, but at least I've the sense not to ask too many questions of a shipful of smugglers."

"Smugglers!" Nyctasia was shocked. Smugglers were the bane of the Maritime cities. As Rhaicime of Rhostshyl it was her duty to see the lot of them arrested, and instead she found herself in league with them.

"Use your sense. Who else would smuggle us out of Chiastelm?"

"Small wonder they don't like questions, then," Nyctasia admitted. "Corson, what does it mean to keelhaul someone?"

Corson succinctly described the brutal punishment. "It's murder, really. No one survives it." She grinned at Nyctasia's discomfiture. "But Destiver's all talk and swagger—she's not about to keelhaul anyone. She'd simply cut our throats and throw us overboard. Just keep out of her way. I've not saved your worthless life twice over just so that you could be food for the fish."

"As to that," said Nyctasia, "why did you save my worthless life a second time? You owed me no further service once we'd reached Chiastelm."

Corson was taken aback. "Why? Well, because . . . you'd not paid the rest of my fee. And you still haven't," she added.

"And I thought," said Nyctasia in wounded tones, "that it was for loyalty and friendship's sake. You like me—admit it!"

Corson flushed. "Like you!" she blustered. "Plague take you! You silly, conceited, devious, high-born witch!"

Nyctasia sat back, helpless with laughter. She was the most irritating person Corson had ever met. You couldn't argue with her, she was too glib. And you couldn't fight with her, she was too small. To get the better of her somehow was a constant challenge to Corson.

"But you're right," Nyctasia said when she'd caught her breath, "I do owe you the rest of your fee." She picked up her cloak from the floor and shook it out. "And an Edonaris always pays her debts." She suddenly ripped one of the patches from the cloak and removed the gemstone concealed beneath it. "Will this suffice?" she asked, tossing the large, brilliant diamond to Corson.

Abashed, Corson stared at the priceless jewel. "Won't you need this? You're a fugitive—how will you pay your way?"

"I only have to go as far as Hlasven. I'll not want for anything with 'Ben."

"Ben?" It was a commoner's name. "I thought he'd have forty names and a score of titles, like you."

"Not quite like me, but you're near the mark. He's the Lord Erystalben Cador Jhaice brenn Rhostshyl ar'n Shiastred. Unless you care to hear the ancillary distinctions as well?"

"Spare me," said Corson. "But what makes you so free with your answers this morning? It's not like you to give names and destinations."

"I'd have to tell you sooner or later, since I assume you're coming with me."

"Why? You won't need a bodyguard once we've landed in Lhestreq."

Nyctasia shrugged. "You've no other plans at present, and I could profit from a few lessons in swordfighting. Besides, I enjoy your company."

Corson didn't know whether to be flattered or indignant. Nyctasia was probably laughing at her. "I may as well go that way as another," she said finally, pocketing the splendid diamond. "I suppose I owe you that much if I take this in fee."

"Nonsense—you've more than earned it. And there's something more due to you as well." She took the golden earrings from her pouch and pressed them into Corson's hand. "Do try not to lose this pair."

Corson was no longer surprised by anything Nyctasia did. She accepted the gift coolly and put them on.

"I was right," said Nyctasia, "they do bring out the gold in your hair. Now we're quits."

"Not quite. There's still something I owe you."

"What's that?"

For answer, she suddenly caught Nyctasia up in her arms and laid her down on the berth.

"Corson—"

Corson knelt beside the berth, bending over her. "Don't be afraid," she teased. "I'm casting a spell on you."

Nyctasia put her arms around Corson's neck and started unpinning the long braid. "Don't you know, a witch whose passions are aroused may turn into a ravening demon?"

"Oh, hold your tongue for once!" Corson exclaimed, and silenced her with a long, fierce kiss.

* * *

It was past noon when Nyctasia emerged from below deck, and the midday meal was almost over. She looked suspiciously at a thick grey soup, consisting mainly of lentils and rubbery potatoes, with an occasional shred of meat which she did not attempt to identify. She had found the food on board ship nearly as bad as Corson had described it, but she was too hungry to be particular. Hard bread and dried apples, with a cup of dark ale, completed the meal. Nyctasia took everything and joined Corson on the long bench.

"*Now* we're quits," Corson remarked smugly.

Nyctasia glanced at her, suppressing a smile. "You're a dangerous woman," she said, biting off a piece of stale bread.

Corson grinned into her soup. "Especially when I'm bored." She wolfed down the rest of her food. "By the way, what does *isnathon scrathling* mean?"

"Corson!" Nyctasia choked on her bread.

"What's the matter?" asked Corson innocently. "You kept saying it to me this morning."

"I called you *that?*"

"And a lot of other things I've never heard before. What does it mean?"

Nyctasia shook her head. "I'm afraid it's quite impossible to translate—"

"Try."

"Really, I . . ." Nyctasia protested, giggling. Corson couldn't get another word out of her for the rest of the meal.

23

THAT NIGHT NYCTASIA could not fall asleep. The cabin seemed more dank and close than ever, and she understood why most of the crew slept on deck in mild weather. "Why should I suffocate in here?" she asked herself. "Even a lady has to breathe." She went above and moved about silently, stepping over sleeping sailors, until she found Corson sprawled by the windlass.

"Oh, it's you," said Corson sleepily. "What did it mean, what you called me?"

Nyctasia lay down beside her. "Go back to sleep."

"Rutting bitch," said Corson. She threw one arm over Nyctasia and promptly fell asleep again.

But Nyctasia was still wakeful. She lay for a long time looking up at the stars and listening to the mysterious creaking and sloshing sounds of the ship. The strong smell of resin and brine was almost as soothing to her as the scent of Maegor's spices, but sleep did not come, and finally she detached herself from Corson and rose. Corson mumbled an incoherent protest and turned away, sighing in her sleep.

Nyctasia wandered restlessly up to the bow and climbed into the forecastle to look out across the sea. A horizon unbounded by city walls was a novelty she never tired of contemplating.

Someone was there before her, leaning on the rail, watching the water. Nyctasia wondered what the night watch on board ship kept guard against. "A fine night," she said politely. "May I join you?"

He turned toward her and bowed. "I should be honored, Rhaicime."

Nyctasia was startled to be addressed by her title of rank—the crew knew who she was, then. But she had paid well for their silence, and Corson claimed they could be trusted.

She stood her ground but remained wary. "You have the advantage of me, sailor," she said evenly.

"Oh, I am but a passenger like yourself, my lady. We have met once before in Rhostshyl, though you've no doubt forgotten."

She could not see his features clearly in the darkness, but it was this very obscurity which seemed somehow familiar. And his voice . . . of course, this was Erystalben's messenger! Now completely at her ease, she joined him at the rail, leaning into the fresh breeze. "Certainly I remember. Have you another letter for me?"

"No, but I bring you a riddle. I am told that you enjoy them." He paused. "Which is the greater power, Lady Nyctasia, the Indwelling or the Invited?"

Nyctasia smiled, thinking of the hours she and 'Ben had spent in arguing this question, trying to reconcile the two. "I will tell you that," she said, "if you can tell me which is the greater—wind or water."

He nodded thoughtfully. "A good answer."

"It is the only answer."

"No question has only one answer. You who are Mistress of Ambiguities must know that."

It was one of 'Ben's nicknames for her. Hearing it, Nyctasia was pierced with longing for him.

"A hand without a weapon may be weak," she said slowly, "but a weapon without a hand is useless."

"Thus, *vahn* is the greater power."

The Mistress of Ambiguities shook her head. "Yet those who are unarmed will fall before swords."

Both were silent for some moments, and Nyctasia suddenly realized how tired she'd become.

"Then there is no answer?" he said at last.

"I have given you two." Nyctasia yawned. "And I fear I'm too weary to devise a third tonight. But I expect we shall meet again."

"I hope so, my lady."

He continued to look out over the dark water. Nyctasia returned to Corson's side and fell asleep at once.

Over the next few days she made certain to speak to every man on board, but none of them sounded like Erystalben's nameless messenger.

Finally, she questioned the captain, who denied having any other passengers on board. "... and the only reason I don't have you two thrown overboard is that we'll reach Lhestreq in two days anyway. And you can tell that rutting friend of yours to stop looking at me like she means to cut my throat!"

Nyctasia was bewildered. "I hadn't noticed that she does. I'll ... er ... speak to her about it."

"You do that," said Destiver and stalked away.

Corson was nowhere on deck, but Nyctasia soon found her in the cabin, sitting on the berth, her head in her hands.

"Feeling bored?" Nyctasia suggested. She sat down and put her arm around Corson's waist. Corson only shook her head without looking up.

"What's the matter with you? The captain says you want to murder her."

"Let me be, can't you?"

Nyctasia began to rub her back and shoulders. Corson shrugged stiffly. "Do that up higher," she said grudgingly. "My head hurts." She hated to admit to any sort of weakness.

"Is that all? Poor thing!" Nyctasia knelt on the berth and started kneading the muscles of Corson's neck. "We'll be in Lhestreq in just two days," she remarked.

"I know."

"Do you know the city well?"

"Of course. I've been there many times."

"And I've never been this far from Rhostshyl in my life."

"Asye! How did you stand it? I left Torisk when I was little more than a child, and I've never been back."

"Where is Torisk? I've never heard of it."

"South," Corson said grimly. "Far south. No one's ever heard of it, it's mostly swamp."

"Ah, that explains it."

"Explains what?" Corson bristled.

"Did you think I meant your manners? Nothing could explain your manners! I was curious about the name   it's very like the word for 'bog' in Ancient Eswraine. Words for features of the land often stay the same, even when—"

Corson was in no mood for one of Nyctasia's lectures. "What of your own name?" she interrupted. "They make an Edonaris wine in the valley lands. I've never had it, it's too costly, but it's famous in the east. They say the same family's made it for centuries. Are you kin to them?"

"I don't know . . . it's the first I've ever heard of them. But it's just possible," Nyctasia mused. "A remote ancestor of mine married into a family of foreign merchants who dealt in fine wines. It was a monstrous scandal, of course. He went with them when they returned to their own country, and they could never trade the coastal markets after that, for fear of the Edonaris. His name was stricken from the family records—I only came upon the story by chance in an old chronicle. If these people are his descendants, they'd be my distant cousins. Perhaps I'll write them a letter."

Corson was disappointed. She'd hoped Nyctasia would take offense at the suggestion that these common vintners were her relations. "My manners are good enough for the company of a wine seller's daughter," she taunted.

"You malign a respectable trade," said Nyctasia.

Corson looked back at her over her shoulder. "What does *isnathon scrathling* mean?" she demanded.

24

LHESTREQ WAS A good-sized port town with a thriving merchant community. There was nothing to distinguish it from any of a dozen similar cities along the coast, but to Corson and Nyctasia it seemed a haven of comfort and luxury after their stay on the *Windhover*. As they ambled through the marketplace on their way to find lodgings, they were enticed by the odors of pastries and cooking meats.

A child ran up to them holding a tray heaped with dates, figs and dried honeyed apricots, all stuffed with nuts. "Buy a sweet, two for a copper!"

Their hands were soon full of sticky fruit, hot meatcakes and small sausages. They ate oranges, sweet buns and gingerbread. "I haven't felt this good for days," Corson said through a mouthful of pastry.

"I thought you must be sick—you'd stopped complaining about the ship's food."

"It was the ship's food making me sick."

"We'll both be sick if we keep this up," said Nyctasia happily. She daintily licked the last sticky crumbs from her fingers. "I have never in my life needed a bath so badly. I stink. So do you, for that matter."

"What?" said Corson absently. Her attention had been caught by a display of glittering jewelry and trinkets. She wandered over to the stall and began covetously fingering the golden chains and gaudy ornaments. She held up a glass bracelet, admiring the way it sparkled in the sunlight. "What do you think of this?" she asked Nyctasia.

"It's a vulgar piece of trash, unworthy to adorn your lovely wrist. Stop pawing through that rubbish and let's find an inn. You know the city, where do you usually stay?"

"Oh, you don't want to stay *there,*" laughed Corson. "And neither do I, not when I have money." She reluctantly laid down the bracelet and pointed across the square. "There's a place up that way, on High Street, that caters to the quality. I've never had the price of a room there, but now I want their best."

She led the way, stopping every few feet, distracted by a new array of tempting wares. Buckles, copper pots, bolts of bright cloth—Corson wanted everything she saw, and it was some time before Nyctasia could pry her away from the marketplace.

When they entered The Crown and Peacock, the patrons, mostly well-to-do merchants, glanced at one another uneasily. Corson and Nyctasia looked more like the class of people who went to the kitchen door asking for work than those who came to the front door seeking accommodations. They were ragged and filthy and didn't look as though they had a copper between them. Obviously troublemakers.

"We want a room," said Corson, banging her fist on a table.

A portly, well-dressed man approached, regarding them with disapproval. "Our rooms are all taken," he said. "Perhaps down the street. . . ."

Corson smiled. She opened the pouch at her belt and pulled out a few gold coins, tossing them in her palm. "A large room," she continued. "The best you have."

The owner bowed. He classed Corson as a soldier fresh from a successful campaign. Nyctasia he dismissed as a penniless student whom the other had undoubtedly picked up for the night. Students as a class were notorious whores.

He waved a servant over. "Show them the corner room upstairs. Lay on fresh bedding. Is there anything else you require?" he asked, turning back to Corson.

"I want a bath," Nyctasia put in. "Hot water, and plenty of it. And something clean to wear."

The innkeeper looked at Corson inquiringly.

"It's all right," she said, with a sweeping gesture. "Get her anything she wants." She grinned at Nyctasia, who suddenly flushed as she realized how things appeared. Swallowing her pride, she meekly followed Corson upstairs.

Corson was delighted with the room. It was large and well-aired, with windows looking on the courtyard and the street. The bed was wide, with an oaken chest at its foot, and a table and two chairs stood at the hearth. There was even a sheepskin rug. Corson fell onto the bed and sank into the down mattresses, laughing.

"Get your boots off the bed," said Nyctasia.

"A little more respect from you, slut. I'll have you thrown into the street, where you belong, if you don't behave."

Nyctasia sighed. "I'm glad you're enjoying yourself."

Corson pulled off her boots and dug her toes into the rug. "I've always wanted to have my way in a grand place like this."

Nyctasia did not see fit to remark that, compared with her apartments in the palace of the Edonaris, this place was a kennel. She possessed to a high degree the aristocratic knack of making herself comfortable anywhere. And the room was reasonably clean. "It's a great deal better than the ship," she said.

Two servants soon came in, carrying a large wooden tub. They were followed by a girl with an armload of clothes.

"Some of these should fit you," she said to Nyctasia, dropping her bundle on the table. She turned to Corson. "Did you want something to wear as well, mistress? We've nothing to hand really big enough for you, but we can wash your clothes tonight and have them dry by morning. Perhaps you could use this?" She lay out a large, shapeless smock on the bed. "They're heating up the bath water now." The girl curtsied to Corson and withdrew.

"Bring me some ale," Corson called after her. She lay back on the bed and stretched luxuriously. "Let's stay here for a while," she suggested. "I want to visit some friends in town, settle an old debt. Maybe buy a few things."

Nyctasia picked out a grey shift from the pile of clothes and examined it dubiously. "Stay if you like. I'll be off to Mehomne as soon as I can get some decent clothing, and a horse. I hope to be in Hlasven in a fortnight."

"You can't," said Corson. "It takes at least a month to travel around Yth Forest."

"I daresay it does, but I mean to travel through it, not around it."

Corson sat up and stared at her. "No one goes through the Yth without need—it's too dangerous. If you've not seen your blue-eyed friend in all this time, you can wait another few weeks, surely!"

"There's a road running through the forest," Nyctasia protested. "Some merchants take it, to reach the eastern markets ahead of the rest."

"I know that, and the greedy bastards usually lose a few people along the way. Don't you know that wood is haunted?"

"Corson," Nyctasia said patiently, "I want to go through the Yth *because* I know it's haunted."

"I should have known," groaned Corson, lying back again. "I hate magicians." She glared balefully at the ceiling.

"Perhaps you really should stay here," Nyctasia said hesitantly. "You certainly won't like—" She stopped abruptly as the servants returned with kettles of steaming water and began to fill the tub. "Tell them to start heating up more," she instructed. "We'll want at least another tubful." She had soon forgotten all else in the soothing luxury of the bath.

Corson dried her hair before the fire, trying to comb out the worst of the snarls. She cursed and yanked at a tangled knot, then gave up and left the comb stuck there while she reached for the mug of ale on the hearthstone.

"Do you want some help?" Nyctasia offered. She was lying across the bed with the contents of her pouch scattered before her. She toyed with a crystal pendant, then picked out a pair of silver, crescent-shaped earrings and put them on. There was a knock on the door.

"Shall we take away the bath now?"

At a nod from Nyctasia, they dragged the tub to the window and tipped it out over the courtyard. The serving-girl came in for their clothes.

"Have these burned," said Nyctasia imperiously. "And have the best tailors in the city here first thing in the morning to take my measurements." Her voice had taken on the assured tone of one accustomed to giving orders. Barefoot, and dressed in the plain grey shift, she nevertheless conveyed the air of a great aristocrat.

"Yes . . . um . . . my lady," said the girl, bewildered. "Will there be anything else?"

Nyctasia considered. "I'll give you a letter to deliver to the moneydealer Eisatt on Bow Street. Fetch me paper and sealing wax, child." She held out a coin. "That will be all."

"Yes, m'lady. Thank you, m'lady." The girl had made up her mind about Nyctasia. She could hardly wait to tell them downstairs.

"Bow Street?" Corson asked suspiciously. "I thought you said you'd never been here before."

"I haven't, but my agents have. I've had this journey planned for a long time, you know." She came over and stirred up the fire. Plucking the comb from Corson's unruly hair, she began to gently smooth out the stubborn tangles.

"Even when you play the great lady you don't mean it," said Corson. "It's just another act. You don't fool me."

Next morning she watched, fascinated, as Nyctasia matter-of-factly gave instructions to tailors and seamstresses while concluding her business arrangements and eating a large breakfast at the same time.

Corson's clothes were stiff and uncomfortable from drying before the fire all night. When Nyctasia dismissed the tailors, she beckoned to one of them herself. "You can take *my* measurements now," she said grandly.

25

IT WOULD TAKE at least two days to complete their garments, and Nyctasia spent most of the time pacing and planning, impatient to be on her way. But Corson would have been contented to spend the whole season at Lhestreq. She made the most of the opportunity to renew old acquaintances and flaunt her unwonted wealth. Sauntering into The Wanton Mermaid one afternoon, she threw down a handful of silver and called for ale all around.

There were only a few idlers there to take advantage of her hospitality. The Wanton Mermaid did most of its business after dark.

"Corson!" The host, a small, canny fellow known as Cricket, threw his arms around her enthusiastically. "I'd given up hope of ever seeing you again—my heart was broken. You owe me thirty crescents."

Cricket owed his success as a taverner to three inviolable rules: He never watered his ale, he never betrayed a secret, and he never forgot a debt. Eyeing Corson's silver skeptically, he picked up a coin and weighed it in his hand.

"Satisfied?" laughed Corson. "It's not false."

"Ah, the girl's picked a rich pocket," said Dorrit, a dark, thin woman who eked out a living as a petty thief.

"This money's honestly come by, Dorrit. I've come up a good deal since you saw me last. I know folk in high places nowadays."

"The gallows . . . ?" suggested Dorrit. Cricket snorted.

"I'm the traveling companion of a great lady, a Rhaicime!"

Corson continued. "She's very elegant, and a scholar too—"

"Who'd you kill, Corson?" Cricket interrupted.

"Here, if you don't believe me, look at these earrings."
She bent toward Dorrit. "She gave them to me, just because
she enjoys my company."

Dorrit touched one wistfully. "These are really valuable,
Corson. They're old."

Cricket whistled. "Sweet Asye! She's killed a Rhaicime!
We'll probably all be hung."

Corson hit the table with her fist. "I told you that—"

"Don't be so touchy, pet. Since you're in such favor with
the nobility, no doubt you can pay me those thirty crescents,
eh?" He winked at Dorrit.

"That's what I've come for." Corson began to count out
coins from her pouch.

Cricket leaped to his feet, astonished. "Not here!" he said,
looking around anxiously. "Let's go in back."

"Watch out, Cricket," Dorrit called after them. "You don't
want to end up owing her. She fetches a high price these
days!"

Cricket barred the door behind them and dragged the mon-
eybox out from beneath his cot. Corson sat on a stool and
watched him unlock the chest with one of the keys at his belt.
When it was safely stored away again she rose to go, but
Cricket caught her hand. "Why so hasty, Corson?" he grinned.
"No time for old friends now that you're the favorite of Rhai-
cimes?"

Corson made an insulting gesture with her free hand. "It's
true, all the same," she insisted.

"Then let's celebrate your good fortune." He hugged her
hard. "I love tall women," he sighed, nuzzling her breasts.

Corson smiled down at him. "But you know I don't like
short men."

"Well, I'm not short all over, pet," said Cricket.
"Remember . . . ?"

26

CORSON WAS FLUSHED and rather unsteady on her feet when she returned to The Crown and Peacock that evening. Nyctasia was at the table, reading by candlelight. "You look like you've had a good time," she observed.

Corson sat down, leaning her head on her hand. "I'm not drunk."

"No?"

"I don't know what's wrong with me these days," Corson complained, shaking her head. "One moment I feel fine, then I'm dizzy and my head aches. I must be getting the grippe. I'm going to bed." She sounded quite sober.

"Don't you even want some supper?"

Corson pulled off her boots and climbed into the bed, drawing the covers over her. "I'm not hungry."

"This sounds serious," said Nyctasia. She sat on the bed and leaned over Corson. "You do look feverish."

Corson's forehead was beaded with sweat. "I'm freezing. It's too cold in here."

Nyctasia frowned. If anything, the room was rather too warm. She went to the table and wrote out a list of simples, then summoned a servant. "Take this to an apothecary's immediately," she instructed, wrapping the paper around some coins, "and bring me a pitcher of strong red wine when you return. Hurry."

"I know an excellent remedy for fever," she assured Corson.

"Does it have bloodroot in it?" Corson asked, suspicious.

"No, why?"

Corson mumbled something and turned away.

When the servant returned, Nyctasia measured out small amounts of the dried herbs and mixed them in a cup of wine which she held over the fire with tongs. "Drink this," she ordered, bringing Corson the hot, fragrant drink.

Corson sipped at it warily. "This is good!" She swallowed it greedily and handed the empty mug back to Nyctasia. "Give me some more."

Corson slept through the evening and late into the following morning. When the tailors arrived to do a first fitting, she felt quite well again, as hungry as ever, and excited at the prospect of her new clothes. She'd never before had clothing made for her, nor had she possessed any of such fine quality. The garments provided by her employers had generally been plain, sturdy goods, which had already seen much use.

The tailors and apprentices flattered her and called her "madame." She was draped in new lambskin and linen which they deftly pulled into place, snipping and stitching, as they turned Corson about and fussed with the materials. She twisted and laughed under their prodding, enjoying herself thoroughly. It took half the time to fit Nyctasia.

Though she fretted about the delay all the next day, at the final fitting Nyctasia had to admit that the results were worth the wait. She had commissioned a suit of plain traveling clothes of a serviceable grey stuff, as well as an elegant outfit of black velvet with silver trimmings. She admired her reflection in the tailors' glass as they made a few final adjustments on the soft, svelte doublet. "Quite satisfactory," she said, smiling. She was equally at home in fine clothes or in her shabby students' garb, but the graceful tailored black was undeniably becoming.

But it was Corson who was really transformed. Instead of a bedraggled layabout, she seemed a young noblewoman dressed for the road. In clothing cut to her measure, her naturally proud carriage and statuesque beauty were set off to the fullest advantage. She wore a close-fitting tunic of fine lambskin over a russet linen shirt, open at the throat, with the full sleeves gathered at the wrist. Her leggings were made of a soft, dark suede.

She stretched like a cat and turned before the mirror, trying to see herself from all sides. "Do I look all right?" she asked anxiously.

Nyctasia broke into astonished laughter.

Corson's face fell. "What's the matter?"

"Do you look all right? Are you blind? You look like sunrise over the rippling wheat! You look like a pillar of golden flame! You look like a fountain of topaz and amber! Corson—yes, you look all right."

27

NYCTASIA TRAVELED ALONE to Mehomne. On the morning of her departure, Corson did not even get out of bed. "You can get yourself eaten by werewolves if you like," she said. "Only a fool would cross the Yth without need."

"Your concern for me is most touching," Nyctasia said cheerfully, pulling on her traveling clothes. "I'll be grieved to part with you, but I suppose I must bear it somehow." In truth, she was rather relieved at Corson's decision. Where Nyctasia was bound, Corson's company might well be more of a hazard than a help. The dangers of the Yth could not be met with a sword. "According to the most respected authorities, werewolves do not eat human beings," she remarked. "They're said to regard it as a sort of cannibalism."

"If the werewolves don't kill you something else will."

"I never said they don't kill people, I said they don't eat them."

Corson raised herself on one elbow. "Nyc, do you know what you're doing?"

Nyctasia perched on the edge of the bed and tugged on her boots. After a moment's thought, she said, "*Yth* means magic, did you know that? 'Yth Wood' wasn't really a name at first —it simply meant, 'the enchanted forest.'"

"Interesting," said Corson, "but not an answer to my question."

"Patience, if you please. I can explain. Do you remember when I told you that magic is a difficult art, that it takes time and study to effect the simplest spell . . . ?"

115

"You were lying?" asked Corson without the slightest surprise.

"Well, not altogether. The power of the *vahn* is only won
through toil and discipline, as I said, and it is limited by one's
own strength. My power is slight because my spirit is weak
and undisciplined.

"But, *yth* is that power drawn from outside oneself—from
sources so much greater than the paltry human spirit!" She
began to pace about the room excitedly, and Corson thought
she must be telling the truth. Nyctasia was always quite at her
ease when she was lying.

"You remember the sea spell I tried when we walked to the
Windhover?"

"I remember that you half-killed yourself with it!"

"*Yth* can be dangerous and unpredictable. I tried to take
power away, to make it part of myself when I was not part of
it . . . You see, a spell of Perilous Threshold draws upon the
power of *yth* swiftly—there's no chance to prepare oneself. It
must be done blindly, without knowing what the cost will be,
and one can only hope that the power will be worth the price.
It's a reckless measure—I only tried it because I was desperate. Oh, I asked little enough, so the risk was not very great;
but if much is demanded, the sacrifice to Balance may be
anything—even life itself."

"And the forest?" Corson prompted her.

"The forest was called Yth because it is a source of magic
—a source that can be drawn upon if one knows the way."

"And at what price?"

"When nothing is taken away, there is nothing to pay.
When nothing is lost what is the cost? What does a mill wheel
take from a river? Turn as it may, there is yet as much water as
ever."

"Rhymes and riddles!" said Corson with contempt.

"Corson, I am trying to answer you. Don't you see, I have
nothing to fear from the Yth because the power belongs to
those who belong to it. It cannot be a danger to itself."

"You can't mean to become part of that cursed forest!"

"No one can become one with the Yth itself and remain
human . . . but there are places near the forest so steeped in its
Influence that those who hold them have vast powers at their
command."

"So that's where you're going. Not to Hlasven."

"I don't know exactly where I'm going, yet, but Hlasven is the nearest place with a name. The land belongs to 'Ben now —or he to it. When I've joined him that power will be mine as well, and we shall both be stronger."

"But only as long as you stay there?"

"If we left, we would lose the land to others, as the mage Vhar Kastenid lost it to 'Ben. There are those now who would wrest it from him if they could—Kastenid himself has tried to reclaim it more than once." She shrugged. "If you would have a water wheel, you must dwell at a river, but a miller doesn't think that a sacrifice."

Corson was dismayed at the idea of being bound to one place for any reason. "It's madness! You'll be the prisoner of your own power!"

Nyctasia smiled. "I shall be free, for the first time in my life." She bent over Corson and kissed her. "And if you're ever bored, you'll know where to look for me."

"I'll remember that," said Corson, turning away and pulling the bedclothes over her head. She heard Nyctasia laugh and heft her satchel onto her shoulder, then close the door and start down the stairs.

Corson tried to sleep. She told herself that she was well rid of Nyctasia, that there was no reason to follow the witch any further. Not even to herself would she admit that she felt too weak to make the journey.

It was no great distance to Mehomne, and Nyctasia made the journey in two days. She rode at a leisurely pace and spent the night at a farmhouse along the way. There was no need to hurry, no need to look behind her. She felt that she was no longer running away, but traveling toward her destination.

It was midday when she reached the city and made her way to The Crossroads Inn. According to 'Ben's directions, this was the usual place to join a party of travelers bound for Yth Forest.

But the news at The Crossroads was disappointing. It might be a fortnight yet before their departure, since they were still too few in the company. Nyctasia only made the ninth, and no one would venture into the Yth with fewer than twenty together.

Nyctasia resigned herself to the wait, but found that her companions at the inn were either unfriendly or too friendly to suit her. She would have been graciously received by any of the local nobility, as a courtesy due to one of her rank, but she was unwilling to make herself known, even this far from Rhostshyl. The habit of secrecy was too strong for her and made her prefer the obscurity of the inn, though she had to share a room with a dealer in silks and spices, who talked too much, and snored. She found herself missing Corson. Corson snored too, but she was never boring.

Nyctasia had no preparations to make in Mehomne, so she spent her time exploring the city, an amusement which soon wore thin. Mehomne was only a stopping place for travelers on their way inland, mainly tradesfolk carrying goods from up and down the coast. When Nyctasia visited the marketplace, she was pestered by a swarm of beggar-children who knew her for an aristocrat as surely as if she were attended by a large retinue. They could seldom be deceived on such a point, which was one reason that Nyctasia had often employed their like as spies. Scattering a handful of coins among them, she escaped into the crowd. Though Nyctasia had long dreamt of traveling far from Rhostshyl, it seemed to her now that all cities were much the same.

"There you are at last, Lady!" said a voice just behind her. "I've been waiting for you. Don't you know the danger—"

Nyctasia turned quickly, her hand on her sword hilt, and found herself facing a thin man wearing three hats, one on top of another, and carrying a long pole hung with a score of others. " . . .the danger of walking bareheaded in the sun?" he continued. "Now, ever since I made this hat I've been waiting for you to come along and buy it. Anyone could see that it was made for you alone." He deftly unhooked a broad-brimmed, grey hat from the pole and handed it to Nyctasia with a bow, somehow contriving not to lose any of the hats he was wearing.

She stroked the black plume pinned to the hat with a silver clasp. Nyctasia could be something of a dandy when she had the leisure. "How much?"

"Five silver crescents, mistress, since I've been saving it specially for you. I could have sold it a dozen times, but it would be a crime to let anyone else have it."

"I'll give you four because I won at dice last night," said Nyctasia. "The hat isn't worth so much, of course, but the performance certainly is."

Her offer was promptly accepted—the hatter would have been glad to get three—and Nyctasia strolled off, equally pleased with the bargain.

"Perhaps some new boots," she thought, but that could wait. Her instinctive lie about the gambling had put her in mind of another errand. She made her way to the artisans' quarter and soon found a goldsmith's shop. There was no mistaking the sign, with its great golden sun and stars.

As she entered the shop, the goldsmith turned from the fire holding a small crucible with slender tongs, and carefully poured the molten gold into a clay mold. A young apprentice laid aside the bellows, brushing the hot hair back from his face with one ringed hand. Both he and the smith were covered with golden jewelry and trinkets. Their bare arms were decked with golden bracelets, and bright pendants swung from their ears. There were gold beads threaded in their hair, and even the heavy work aprons were stitched with flat stars of gold foil.

The apprentice came up to Nyctasia. "How may we serve you, mistress?" he asked politely.

Nyctasia shielded her eyes, as if dazzled by his glittering splendor. "Well, I was wanting a locket, but perhaps I'll buy you instead."

The boy chuckled. "I daresay Desskyres would gladly sell me, but I'll fetch some lockets for you anyway, shall I?" He set a stool at the table for Nyctasia and went into the back room of the workshop.

The smith, Desskyres, eyed Nyctasia with unconcealed interest and smiled, revealing a gold tooth. "You can have him for a copper penny and welcome, lady! In truth, I'd pay you to take him off my hands."

The boy reappeared with a tray, which he set before Nyctasia. "That one mistreats me something dreadful," he told her in a loud whisper. "Starves me and beats me—it's a wonder I can stand!"

"You look like it," laughed Nyctasia.

Like the rest of the marketfolk, these two took her for a trader—as she intended—and called her 'lady' simply to flatter her. Had they guessed at her real title, neither would have dared to joke or flirt with her.

She was intrigued by the pair—and especially by the beautiful, dark-skinned smith. She could hardly take her eyes from those lean, muscled arms, ringed with gleaming gold.

Glancing at the tray of jewelry, she saw what she wanted at once. "This one," she said, holding up a highly polished, heart-shaped locket. "This is perfect."

The smith came over to inspect her choice and nodded approval. "That's a fine piece of work. Feel how smooth it is—burnished with soft sand for hours. It's costly, you know."

Nyctasia only smiled. "Can you engrave a name on it?"

"Surely. Write it out, if you will."

The apprentice fetched a slate covered with designs and words, and offered Nyctasia a piece of chalkstone. She handed the locket to Desskyres, letting her fingers brush lightly across the smith's warm palm. Then, taking up the stone, she scratched out, "MELLIS."

"That's easily done," said Desskyres. "I could have it ready tomorrow, if need be. Or the next day."

"There's no great hurry—just let me know when it's finished. I'm staying at The Crossroads."

The smith frowned. "*Vahn,* lady, you don't want to go among such people. Criminals, the lot of them!"

"Indeed?"

"Don't you know? That's where folk gather who want to travel through the Yth. Who'd be so desperate as that if they weren't pursued for some crime?"

"I would, for one," Nyctasia said mildly.

"Are you mad?" the smith cried, then looked at her sharply, "or are you a witch?"

"Oh, a bit of both, perhaps. But what of you—are you a man or a woman? I've been wondering all this while."

The apprentice snickered. "A bit of both, perhaps?" he suggested.

"Clear those things away!" ordered the smith. "And go buy some lamb's wool. I told you yesterday we've need of more."

"I'm going!" The boy winked at Nyctasia and went out.

Desskyres sat on the table, leaning toward Nyctasia. "As to your question, pretty one, if you were very curious, I could suggest an excellent way for you to find out."

"A fair answer," murmured Nyctasia. She too leaned forward, tracing one finger along the prominent cheekbone that reminded her of Erystalben's. "Alas that there's no privacy to be had at The Crossroads."

"The Crossroads is no place for you, and neither is the Yth. You'd do better to stay here—you're such a tiny thing you'd not take up much space." The smith's lips brushed her ear, whispering, "I'd make you forget that nonsense about the forest."

Nyctasia shivered. A fortnight in Mehomne no longer seemed such a tedious prospect.

As she left the smithy, Nyctasia met the apprentice returning. He bowed. "What, leaving so soon, mistress? Were you not pleased with our wares?"

"I mean to return later," said Nyctasia, "when I can study them at my leisure."

"You'll not be disappointed. 'Kyres was smitten with you, plain to see! I fear I'll have to sleep on the hearth tonight."

"Not you, lad. I'll wager you have a dozen other lovers who'd be glad to take you in."

"Oh, well, if you've heard my reputation—!" he replied, with a modest shrug. "You mustn't believe all that folk say."

"I believe very little of what I hear," Nyctasia said drily. Reputation indeed, the puppy! All the same, he was nowhere to be seen when she returned that night to the smithy.

The room over the workshop was surprisingly comfortable. The furnishings were dark, carved oak of fine workmanship, and intricately wrought lamps stood on brackets in the corners. One wall was draped with a tapestry of a great tree with bright leaves of all colors.

As Nyctasia admired it, Desskyres came up behind her and clasped her around the waist. "What are you thinking of, little one?"

She leaned back and drew the smith's gold-ringed arms around her. "I was thinking," she lied, "that although I never wear gold, tonight I shall make an exception."

"Never wear gold—what blasphemy under my roof! Then you yourself are not Mellis?"

"By no means. I'm Nyc."

"And who's this Mellis, then?" Desskyres demanded, pretending jealousy.

"Why, no one at all, just a child," said Nyctasia, beginning to unfasten her shirt.

"That's what you like, eh?"

"You're what I like. Whatever you are."

"What would you prefer me to be?" whispered Desskyres, slipping the shirt from Nyctasia's shoulders. "I like to please."

"Hlann! I don't care!" exclaimed Nyctasia. She tilted her head back and kissed the smith under the chin. Strong hands pressed her breasts and gently caught the swelling nipples between thumb and forefinger. Nyctasia drew a sharp breath. Desskyres kissed her temple.

Nyctasia started to turn, but felt a painful tug at her neck. One long, gold earring had caught in the soft hair at her nape. Desskyres carefully pulled it free. "There now."

"Those are dangerous, smith. Traps for the unwary!"

"Of course they are—anyone who wears my jewelry is irresistible." Desskyres laughed and set the gold pendants swinging, burning as they caught the candlelight.

For a moment, the sight struck Nyctasia as strangely familiar . . . then she remembered—Corson, at the inn in Lhestreq, shaking her head in the same way, the candlelight gleaming on the gold Edonaris earrings. But Corson had not laughed. "I don't know what's wrong with me," she'd said. "One moment I feel fine, then I'm dizzy. . . ."

Nyctasia's heart froze in horror. She knew those signs. The headaches, the sudden fever . . . but only now did she realize when they'd *begun*.

Desskyres touched her cheek. "Nyc, what's the matter?"

"No, nothing. I—" Nyctasia began to pull on her shirt.

"Where are you going?! You *are* mad!"

"*Vahn!* I hope so," cried Nyctasia. She flung her arms around the smith for a swift kiss. "I've no time to explain—I'll send a message. I'm so sorry!"

Within a moment she was down the stairs and out of the smithy. Before nightfall the next day she was at the gates of Lhestreq.

28

"WHAT WOULD YOU have me say?" asked the host of The Crown and Peacock. "I know nothing more about it. As I told you, she went on her way days ago." He looked as if he wished that Nyctasia would do the same.

It was not easy to get a lie past a practiced liar like Nyctasia. "I see," she said coldly. "The truth of it is, you threw her out because she was sick." But she could get nothing more from the landlord, and she was at a loss as to where to look next.

As she paced back and forth in front of the shops on High Street, the serving-girl from the inn darted up to her and curtsied hurriedly. "M'lady, you might find her on Cobble Row — there's places there anyone can stay."

"How sick was she?" Nyctasia asked, anxious.

"Well, she could ride, m'lady, but she looked very poorly. The master was afraid to let her stay lest it spread to others."

Nyctasia paid the girl for her information and let her go. She knew now that she must find Corson at all costs. If what she suspected was true, there might not be much time left.

After hours of fruitless inquiry among the denizens of Cobble Row, and a good deal of money wasted on false clues, Nyctasia was discouraged, tired, and no nearer to finding Corson. Only at a seamy tavern called The Wanton Mermaid had anyone even admitted to having seen Corson, but they could not (or would not) tell her anything helpful.

"She said she was staying at the Peacock with a wealthy

Rhaicime," scoffed one of the women. "Of course, nobody believed that. She had plenty of money, though."

Nyctasia had hastily departed, avoiding the curious stares directed her way.

Toward midnight she ordered a meal in a tavern that seemed slightly less squalid than the rest. A large, middle-aged woman was scraping food from the tables and gathering empty mugs while keeping a wary eye on her remaining customers. A young man carried ale and food from the kitchen. Nyctasia paid him, took a few cautious bites of the bread, then gave up all pretense at eating. She laid another coin, a heavy silver Meridian, on the table and addressed the busy woman.

"Perhaps you've seen a friend of mine—a tall swordswoman called Corson, with money to spend—"

"Lady, I get soldiers in here all the time," said the woman impatiently. She did not pick up the coin.

"You'd remember this one—she's beautiful. Bright brown hair in a long braid, and wide blue eyes. She was probably sick, maybe feeling mean...."

"What kind of fool soldier wears long hair?"

Nyctasia sighed. "Vanity makes fools of us all," she said wearily. "You've not seen her then?"

At that, the young man came up to them. "Ma, I'll wager she means the crazy one, over at Merl's."

"I never heard that *she* was beautiful."

He shrugged. "I never heard she wasn't. And she sure is sick. Merl's just waiting for her to die so he can throw her out. Last time he tried, she broke his arm," he told Nyctasia with a giggle.

She stood. "Where is this place?"

"I'll show you," he said eagerly. "It's not far."

The woman pocketed Nyctasia's money. "All right, but bring yourself right back here after. There's work to do."

"That one has to be into everything," she complained, watching them from the doorway. She frowned and suddenly called after Nyctasia, "Lady, don't tell Merl you're a friend of hers!"

* * *

"Has that madwoman upstairs died yet, Merl?" shouted Nyctasia's guide.

"I don't know," growled a heavyset, bearded man with one arm in a sling. "Why don't you go up and look for yourself?"

"I will," said Nyctasia. "Show me where she is." She started up the stairs.

Merl shrugged and followed her, with the youth and a few curious customers trailing after them. "In here," he said. "Watch out, she's rutting dangerous."

The others prudently fell back as Nyctasia went in. She shut the door behind her and hastened to Corson's bedside. "Corson, take off those earrings! That bastard Brethald poisoned them!"

But Corson didn't move. She lay on a dirty straw pallet, her unsheathed sword on the floor at her left hand. Only her labored breathing showed that she was still alive.

Nyctasia knelt beside her and began to draw off the golden earrings but Corson lunged without warning and dragged her to the floor. Before she could call out for help, Corson had her by the throat.

* * *

Corson was back in the woods, surrounded by the band of jeering thieves. "We'll have the jewelry too," said the leader, and reached to take her prized earrings. This time he'd not get the better of her so easily! She threw him to the ground and fell upon him savagely, her hands closing around his throat. But as she stared down into the robber's face, his features began to break and shift like reflections on the surface of a pond. . . .

Nyctasia was unprepared for the attack, and struggled vainly to break Corson's grip. There was a ringing in her ears and dazzling black patches clouded her vision. Desperate, she groped for her dagger but Corson suddenly went limp, overcome by weakness, and collapsed, senseless.

When Nyctasia had somewhat recovered her breath she bent over Corson and listened for her heartbeat, then quickly drew off the earrings, wrapping them in a handkerchief. Satisfied, she got to her feet, still gasping, and went out to the landing.

"Is she dead?" said Merl eagerly.

Nyctasia leaned on the doorframe, one hand to her throat,

and looked at him with disgust. "Get me some rope," she ordered.

With Corson seemingly lifeless, and safely bound, the innkeeper felt much bolder about entering the room. He glared at Nyctasia, who was laying her folded cloak under Corson's head. "She's not staying here!" he said.

Nyctasia stood. "Don't worry, man, it isn't catching. She's not sick, she's poisoned."

"How do you know?"

For answer, Nyctasia unwrapped the glittering earrings. "These were prepared with a deadly poison, but it wasn't intended for her—she stole them. It's unwise to steal from me." The lie would serve as a warning. Nyctasia knew that everyone at the inn probably had plans to rob her already.

Merl looked uneasy. "Well, I don't care what's wrong with her, she's not going to die under my roof. Folk will stay away for a year if they hear about it. You get her out of here or I will."

"She'll not die, I promise you," Nyctasia said, hoping that she spoke the truth. "I'm a healer, I'll see to her."

"She's trouble, dead or alive," said Merl stubbornly.

"Listen to me, man—I don't want her here any more than you do. I'd rather have her someplace clean! But she's too sick to be moved yet, and anyone who tries it will regret it!" She spoke firmly, looking straight at the man like one who can make good her threats. He dropped his eyes. As ever, Nyctasia was convincing.

"I'll take her away when she's stronger," she continued, "but I can make it well worth your while to keep her here for now."

This made a better impression on Merl. "You'll pay what she owes? She broke some furniture too, you know."

"You'll be satisfied." Nyctasia paced rapidly around the room, hands clasped behind her, then pointed to the weapons she'd taken from Corson. "Lock those up somewhere. And have this room cleaned. Thoroughly!"

"How do I know you can do what you say? If she dies—"

Nyctasia smiled. "Very well, you shall have proof." Her face assumed a strange dreamy expression which the burly innkeeper viewed with misgiving. He backed away a step as Nyctasia approached him.

29

CORSON COULD SEE nothing but a thin film of mist that crept around her feet. She tried to struggle, but something held her until she lay with her strength spent, watching as the fog swirled about her knees. It clung to her waist, then moved up over her breasts, and from behind her came a pitiful, low, moaning sound. Her head was held still and something pressed against her lips. Wetness filled her mouth.

She awoke and found Nyctasia standing over her. "Nyc," she whispered, "I have to tell you . . . burning . . . we're burning! Who can help us?" She spoke hurriedly, sure that she had to warn Nyctasia, but to her horror she heard herself babbling nonsense. Nyctasia's face withdrew, retreating farther and farther away until it seemed no nearer than a star in the night sky. Then, there was only darkness. . . .

Once Nyctasia had healed his broken arm, and paid handsomely for Corson's board, Meil was won over and even became helpful. He let it be known at the inn that anyone who troubled Nyctasia would have him to deal with, and he'd see to it that they never again troubled anyone.

Before long, Corson's room was comfortably furnished, though Corson herself was hardly aware of the difference. Still delirious and dangerous, she had to be forced to submit to any care, and to swallow the antidotal potions Nyctasia prepared for her.

Nyctasia kept a constant watch over her, sleeping little, pacing, always reproaching herself. She should have foreseen such a thing! It was intolerable to her that someone else should suffer for her carelessness, that Corson should die like this, not at the hands of enemies, not in fair fight, but by pure mischance!

But it was not only Corson's danger that troubled her—she was haunted by the memory of her henchman, Sandor, as well. He had served her faithfully and risked his life in her service more than once, yet when Thierran had killed him she'd sorrowed less than for a hound lost in the hunt. Sandor had always done his duty, but Nyctasia felt that she had somehow failed in hers. Failed, not only in her duty to Sandor, but to some principle of her own philosophy. Who had killed him, in truth, Thierran or herself? When she tried to think about Sandor, she could hardly recall his face. And now, had Corson too outlived her usefulness?

Surely Corson was different, though. Such a wanton, winning creature with her bold tongue and her reckless courage, her generous laughter and her prickly pride. So quick to take offense, so ready to be cajoled.

But Corson was not so very different from others of her station; rather, Nyctasia was different from the woman she had been. For a Vahnite, there was no forgiveness for an offense against the Indwelling Spirit. One could only make amends by becoming a person who was incapable of such a crime.

Nyctasia had been, by turns, amused and angered by Corson, as she might have been by some half-wild household pet. Now, with a pang, she remembered the ways she had tricked Corson, trapped her, used her. She knew that her servants thought her a just and generous mistress—such was the proper role for an Edonaris. Nyctasia had always performed her part well, but it had never been more than a performance. She was not aware of how much she was changing. She only knew that Corson's death would weigh on her heart as well as her spirit.

Corson whimpered. "Nyc, where are you? There's blood on the sand—" but she did not know that Nyctasia was bending over her, bathing her face with cool water. She was wandering along a beach at dusk, looking for something lost, her feet bare and bleeding. The cold wind from the sea threw spray in her face, and she shivered.

Nyctasia brushed back the damp hair from Corson's hot, fever-flushed face. Corson's magnificent hair was lank and dull now, her skin sallow. It was too late for medicines to save her, the poison had been at work too long—long enough to have killed the small, slight Nyctasia. Had she worn the earrings herself, as Brethald intended, there would not have been time for her to realize what ailed her.

Corson was seized with a fit of trembling, and Nyctasia, still watching her, finally came to a decision. With a determined nod, she rose and barred the door. So be it. She would try to work a healing trance, whatever the risk. It was not a spell she should attempt without help, for Corson was far nearer to death than anyone she had tried to heal before. There should be someone at hand to recall her at the proper time and sever the spell. She thought for a moment of enlisting the aid of Merl, who had become her champion, but she dared not trust his goodwill as far as that. She would be utterly at the mercy of anyone who attended her.

Very well, she must take the chance—not only for Corson's sake, but for her own.

Nyctasia wasted no more time. Sitting on the bed, she unlaced Corson's shirt and placed her hand over Corson's heart. She lowered her head and waited, eyes closed, pacing her thoughts to the measured rhythm of Corson's heartbeat and entering gently into the pattern of the first Recognition, the commencement of the Influence Toward Life.

> Sleeping one, *dream of me*.
> Distant one, *greet me*.
>
> Silent one, *speak to me*.
> Secret one, *heed me*.
>
> Lonely one, *lean to me*.
> Lost one, *seek me*.
>
> Captive one, *reach to me*.
> Fugitive, *flee to me*.
>
> Hider, *draw near to me*.
> Wild one, *be dear to me*.
>
> Stranger, *receive me*.

As the words possessed her, all else receded and became unreal. There was nothing but the seeking in darkness, the reaching of one spirit to another. Then even the words gave way, and only the rhythm remained to guide her. She followed it blindly, trustingly, until she came to its source—the black waves beating on the dark shore.

A still figure lay just out of reach of the breaking waves, and Nyctasia went to her, trying not to see the familiar likeness of Corson, but only to be aware of her presence. The pulse of the surf now said to her, *"Neither land nor sea. Neither earth nor air."* Nyctasia knew that she was here only in spirit, but it was all-important that she not only know this but believe it, not only believe but remember. Remember. Remember that this was not a place but a state of being. Remember that one could not truly be here, that one must not, above all, stay here. . . . Everything that she thought she saw or felt or heard, she must deny.

She would not even think of Corson by name. "Friend," she said, "it is time we were away from here. The tide is coming in." *Neither sea nor sky. Neither shore nor star.*

The being who was Corson and yet was not Corson, replied faintly, "I cannot. I am too weak."

"That is your dream, but I am here to wake you. Arise. You are whole, you are healed."

The only answer was the ghost of a sigh.

"Trust in me, do you not know me?" *Neither lips nor tongue. Neither voice nor word.*

A hesitation. "I . . . know you. . . ."

"And I know you. You are a warrior! This battle is not done yet."

"No. . . ."

"You have only to face the enemy to defeat them. They are mere shadows who war against you. Come away. Lean on me." *Neither hands nor limbs. Neither tears nor blood.*

Together, they moved away from the black waves, Corson's steps growing firmer even as Nyctasia's weakened.

"Don't leave me," Corson cried.

"You can stand alone now," Nyctasia said aloud, but there was no one to hear her. She was kneeling beside the bed where Corson still lay senseless, beyond the reach of her voice. For a long while Nyctasia knelt there, trembling, ashen, unable to rise. Then, gripping the bedstead, she pulled herself to her feet and staggered to her cot, where she lay gasping like a drowning woman.

30

BECAUSE SHE REMEMBERED nothing that she had experienced
during her trance, Nyctasia had no way of knowing whether
she had been successful. Her own weakness told her that she
had given strength to Corson, but had it come in time to shift
the balance towards life? Corson seemed unchanged, still
wandering in her fever dreams, and Nyctasia could only con-
tinue to nurse her and hope for some encouraging sign.

Corson thought that she had been walking for days on end
without finding her way. She longed for rest but felt that she
must keep moving on, though she no longer remembered why.

Then someone called to her, and she saw a tall figure coming towards her over the dunes. "Steifann . . . ?" She tried to
run to him, but soon stopped, exhausted. "Steifann, help me!
I'm so tired . . ." But it was not Steifann who reached to embrace her. Corson frantically felt for her sword, but it had
been lost somehow. She screamed as the grinning spectre bent
over her, sliding its arm around her waist, trying to force open
her mouth with its tongue. Suddenly furious, she struck out
wildly at the creature with all her remaining strength, only to
find herself lying in a strange room, staring at her own hand.
For some reason, a bed slat had been tied to her arm.

Nyctasia scrambled to her feet and ran to throw open the
door so that she could summon help if Corson broke free to
attack her. She watched from a safe distance as Corson tried to
sit up, looking about in bewilderment.

"Steifann . . . ?"

Nyctasia approached cautiously. "It's Nyc."

Corson stared at her. "Why is your shirt all wet?"

"This is the broth I was trying to feed you when you knocked me down just now." She picked up a broken bowl and set it on the table.

"I did not," said Corson. She lay back and tugged at the cord at her other wrist. "Help me!"

Nyctasia hesitated, then sat on the edge of the bed and undid the knots. "Who did this?" Corson demanded, frightened.

"I did. You keep trying to kill me."

Corson looked puzzled. "We have to hurry," she said vaguely. "It's almost dawn." She fell asleep again before Nyctasia could reply.

Nyctasia laid her palm against Corson's temple, and smiled. The fever had broken.

* * *

"I'm not hungry."

Nyctasia sighed. "How in the Hlann's name do you think to get your strength back if you won't eat?" She began to straighten Corson's tangled bedclothes again.

Corson picked unenthusiastically at the plate of stew before her. "It's probably poisoned," she muttered.

But Nyctasia only laughed. "Do you want me to eat some of it first?"

"As soon as I do get my strength back, the first thing I'm going to do is tear you into shreds, you murderous bitch."

"I know, you told me. But last time you mentioned it you were planning to cut out my heart and liver and skewer them. Let me know when you've decided which it's to be."

"I will." She started to eat the stew, which was not at all bad.

Corson was bored with being confined to bed. She'd been trying for days to provoke Nyctasia, but all her threats and insults had been met with a good-humored patience that was driving her mad. She liked Nyctasia better as a sharp-tongued shrew. "What are you doing now?" she demanded.

"Writing a letter."

"Where are my weapons?"

Nyctasia paid no attention. Corson looked for something to

throw at her, but there was nothing at hand except the stew. She hit the wall with her fist.

Nyctasia looked up. "Do you want something, or are you just trying to annoy me?"

Corson didn't know what she wanted. When Nyctasia tried to amuse her, she wanted to be left alone, and when Nyctasia ignored her, she felt neglected. Unused to illness, she had no idea that her despair and frustration were only the aftermath of fever. Suddenly she burst into tears.

Nyctasia went to her and embraced her. "You're a goose! Hush now, listen to me—if you like, I'll . . ." she lowered her voice. "I'll tell you what *isnathon scrathling* means."

Corson grabbed her arm. "Tell me."

Nyctasia whispered something to her and she gasped. "You filthy . . . ! Get away from me!" She kicked out at Nyctasia who backed away and dropped into her chair, laughing.

"I think *I'll* write a letter," Corson announced.

"Very well." Nyctasia cut another sheet from her book and dipped the quill afresh. Writing was a difficult skill, practiced mainly by students and scribes. The wealthy employed secretaries to write their correspondence, and others patronized public scriveners. Nyctasia naturally assumed that Corson meant to dictate the letter to her. "Very well, what do you want to say?"

"No, give it to me. I'll write it myself."

Skeptical, but curious, Nyctasia brought her the book and quill, and sat on the bed to watch, holding the ink.

Corson was clearly a self-taught scribe. As she laboriously dragged the quill over the rough paper, the point frequently caught in the fibre, spattering ink across the page. But Corson persisted. "MY DEAREST STEIFANN," she scrawled.

Nyctasia couldn't bear it. "Corson, that is a pen, not a sword—don't stab the paper with it. Hold it loosely and let it slide over the surface."

"I don't want lessons in penmanship!"

Nyctasia stood. "I'm going out, then. Shall I bring you anything?"

Corson only shook her head, intent on her writing. As soon as Nyctasia was gone, she tried to follow her suggestions—but it only became harder to control the pen. She tore out page after page and used them up, practicing. The point of the quill soon wore down, but there was nothing to sharpen it with.

When Nyctasia returned after an hour, she found Corson hunched scowling over yet another ragged and blotchy effort. Her hand was cramped and ink-stained, and there was a black smear across the bridge of her nose. She crumpled up the page and threw it at Nyctasia. "Let it slide over the surface!" she shouted. "How, curse you?!"

Nyctasia set down her satchel and looked at the mess Corson had made of her commonplace book. It required all her powers of self-discipline just to keep her temper. "I thought you didn't want lessons in penmanship. You should be resting, not wearing yourself out over trifles. Lie down!" To Corson's relief, she cleared the rubbish from the bed and threw it on the fire.

Corson lay back and shut her eyes, too tired even to give Nyctasia an argument. Her own weakness frightened her more than any enemy. How could an hour of sitting up and scribbling be so exhausting? "I'll never be well again!"

"You just need time to mend, that's all. If you'd stop fretting yourself, you'd feel a good deal better. Look——" She reached in her satchel and brought out a matching silver comb and hairbrush. "These are for you. Perhaps they'll keep you amused for a while. After all, you are the vainest person I've ever known."

Corson was already unpinning her braid. She gathered up her hair and drew the brush through it a few times, but even this soon became tiring.

"Shall I do it for you?" Nyctasia offered.

"Mmm, all right." Corson loved to have her hair brushed. She toyed with the silver comb. "These are just of a piece with my mirror. Look in my pack—it's wrapped in a cloth. I meant to leave it with Steifann, but I forgot about it, with all the trouble you caused me."

"Steifann . . . is that your friend the taverner?"

Corson nodded. "Best lover in the land. He arranged the passage for us with that Destiver. 'Old friends,'" she scoffed. "Hah!"

"That's what you had against her!" said Nyctasia, enlightened. "Corson, I don't think you need to worry."

"You don't know Steifann. He'll bed down with anyone."

"Not like you."

"Are you going to brush my hair or aren't you?"

"At once, milady!" She wrapped one long coil of hair around her hand and started to brush it slowly.

"He's probably whoring all over the city by now, and me dying," Corson mourned.

"The women of ancient Kehs-Edre wore a certain perfume in their hair, when they wanted to keep their men in thrall," Nyctasia remarked. "I have the recipe in one of those useless books of mine."

"How can you perfume your hair?"

"Soak a wooden comb in it for three nights and three days, then let it dry. You just comb your hair with it and the scent lingers . . . men can't resist it."

"What a story!"

"It's true, though," said Nyctasia, with the conviction of one who has made the experiment. "In hair like yours, the effect would be maddening. I'll make you a comb like that someday, if you like."

"When?" Corson asked. She began to feel that she might recover after all.

Over the next week Corson's health, as well as her handwriting, made rapid improvement. When several days had passed without a recurrence of the delirium, Nyctasia succumbed to Corson's insistent demands that her weapons be returned.

"Er . . . do you want these back as well?" Nyctasia asked hesitantly, holding out the golden earrings. "I've washed them in vinegar—they're quite safe."

"*You* wear them. If you live long enough, I'll take them back."

"Gold doesn't suit me."

Corson shrugged. "Keep them."

With a sigh, Nyctasia changed her silver earrings for the gold.

31

"YOU'RE RIGHT," SAID Corson, some days later, "they look better on me. Give them back."

They were sitting in The Crossroads in Mehomne, indulging in one of their usual arguments. They had arrived on the eve of a caravan's departure for the Yth, and Corson had been hired by the travelers as an extra guard. It was a job few were willing to undertake, and the wages were more than liberal. Corson felt that the occasion warranted celebration, and she had already downed several tankards of ale.

Nyctasia too was in high spirits. "I've never known a man to equal 'Ben," she said, resuming their earlier discussion. She returned the gold earrings to Corson and put on her silver ones.

"That's because you don't know Steifann. I've had them all—gentlemen, peasants, townsmen—nobody compares with Steifann."

"Nobody . . . ?" said Nyctasia, glancing towards a man who had just entered. Corson turned to look.

The newcomer was a striking, black-skinned man with strong, sharply chiseled features and a powerful, well-knit frame. He was of average height, but his proud, graceful bearing gave him greater stature.

"I see what you mean," said Corson. For once, she and Nyctasia were in complete agreement.

"We could throw dice for him," Nyctasia suggested.

"You'd charm the dice. Let's arm wrestle instead. I'll even use my right hand."

"Thanks, but I'm afraid I'd find it difficult to write with all of my knuckles broken."

"Well, we'll just have to share him, then."

"Done," said Nyctasia.

They were delighted when the stranger, after glancing around the room, came straight to their table. Corson gave him her most winning smile but he only nodded to her, then turned to Nyctasia with a formal bow. "Give you good evening, my lady."

Nyctasia frowned for a moment, but then broke into laughter. "Do sit down, sir," she said graciously. "So you've come into the light at last—it was a shame to hide such beauty in the shadows. Are you still following me?"

"Let us put it that we have the same destination, my lady."

Corson did not care for the turn events were taking. "Why didn't you tell me you knew him?" she demanded.

"I wasn't aware of it till he spoke," Nyctasia explained. "An occasional conversation with an unseen person is not considered a proper introduction. But he's been two steps behind me since before we left Rhostshyl."

"I'd have known if someone was following you!"

"Corson, you are the best of bodyguards, but even you can't watch for shadows in your sleep."

"Another rutting magician!" Corson said with disgust. "They come out of nowhere like maggots these days." She drained her ale and waved for another. "Do you want me to kill him?"

Nyctasia was enjoying herself. "I'm sure that won't be necessary."

"Too sure, perhaps," the stranger interrupted, suddenly abandoning his deference. "You are too sure of a number of things, lady."

Nyctasia leaned back, one eyebrow raised, as she contemplated this insolence. "What is this?" she said slowly, "another riddle?"

"No, a warning." He paused, then exclaimed with vehemence, "You have made sacrifices, Edonaris, but you do not understand that for power one must sacrifice everything!" He did not take his eyes from Nyctasia's, and she returned his stare. Bored, Corson finished her ale.

"What price have you paid for power?" Nyctasia said

sharply. "Why have I never seen you by daylight? Why do you give no name?"

He looked away. "*I* have not given up what was not mine to give."

Nyctasia's grey eyes were the color of steel. "You dare say that I have done so?"

He shook his head. "If I still suspected you, you would never have seen my face. Nor would I risk my life to warn you."

"What is this warning, then?"

"Do not go to Hlasven," he said softly.

"You are no servant of Shiastred!"

"Nor are you, Lady Nyctasia. Not yet."

Nyctasia glared at him in disbelief. "I suppose you bribed 'Ben's messenger to give you the letter?"

He made a gesture of dismissal. "The letter did not interest me. To command a Reflection of the spirit I needed to see you and receive a token from you. This has served my purpose," he said, handing Nyctasia her glove.

"I'm sorry to have put you to such trouble," Nyctasia said coldly. "It would have been easier with a lock of my hair."

"It would have been easier to kill you! I preferred to try the spell. If I'd found you were no different from Shiastred, I'd have used any means to keep you from him. I can't hope to fight both of you."

"You will have to kill me, then."

"We'll see. I don't expect you to believe me now—only listen. When you've learned the truth about Shiastred, come to me."

For answer, Nyctasia threw the glove in his face, and rose to walk away without a word.

The stranger seized her arm. "Hear me—"

Corson had long since stopped listening and devoted herself to her drinking, but suddenly she too was on her feet. Kicking aside her chair, she pulled the man away from Nyctasia and stepped between them, sword in hand. Everyone in the room was watching them by now. "Nyc, do you want me to kill him or not?" she asked reasonably. "Make up your mind."

Nyctasia smiled at her and shook her head.

Corson put up her sword. "Well, what are you lot staring

at?" she inquired of the room at large, and people turned back to their own affairs.

The stranger sighed, rubbing his arm where Corson had twisted it. "My lady, you have nothing to fear from me. Will you not speak to me alone?"

"Very well," Nyctasia said flatly. "I will listen, but I have nothing more to say." She followed him to the door.

"Wait!" Corson protested. "We had an agreement. We're supposed to share him."

Nyctasia glanced back at her. "I'll be back soon. Don't worry."

Corson stared after them, wondering whether she should follow Nyctasia. "That little slut," she muttered, "let her fend for herself. He probably thinks she's a boy, anyway." She consoled herself with more ale and finally staggered off to bed, ignoring with drunken dignity several offers of company for the night.

"Move over!" Nyctasia demanded, trying to shove Corson to one side of the bed.

Corson grunted. "You're back already," she mumbled. "He must have been a disappointment."

"I said move, you overgrown sow!"

"What happened?"

Nyctasia climbed over her. "Go back to sleep. The caravan leaves at sunrise, you know."

"Tell me about him," Corson insisted, still half asleep.

Nyctasia was silent for a time. "I should have let you kill him," she said quietly. "He's Vahr Kastenid."

"What?"

"Go to sleep!"

Corson yawned. "It serves you right," she said with satisfaction.

32

IT WAS A good two days' journey to the marches of the Yth, and the countryside grew ever wilder and more desolate on the way. They made camp early on the second night, at the edge of the wood, refusing to enter the Yth at nightfall. Everyone in the party felt oppressed and uneasy except Nyctasia, who was afire with anticipation. She argued that they would be no safer by day, since the Yth was known to harbor an unvarying twilight at all hours, but the others chose to wait for dawn, nevertheless.

Disappointed and restless, Nyctasia wandered around the camp, listening for sounds from the forest. Finally she came and sat by Corson, who was keeping watch by the campfire.

"Stop prowling about," Corson ordered. "Stay where I can see you."

"Look at this." Nyctasia unclenched her fist, and a small flame appeared, dancing above her open hand as if an invisible wick grew from her palm.

Corson frowned at it. "Magicians!" she said, and spat.

"Must you do that?"

Corson pointed to the eerie flame over Nyctasia's hand. "Must *you* do that?"

"I never could do it before. It's the Influence of the Yth—so close, I've only to reach out for it!" She spoke as if to herself, and Corson looked off into the shadowy forest, ill at ease. Nyctasia had begun to seem a stranger to her.

"You've been different ever since we got near this cursed forest. You act like you're listening to something no one else can hear. I don't like it."

"I do." Nyctasia closed her hand over the flame and it vanished. "You could still turn back. There's no need for you to make this journey."

"I'm being paid handsomely for it—I'll go back to Steifann's with a fortune. I'm not afraid of spirits."

"That's what worries me."

"Your watch is up, Corson." Another guard had arrived to relieve her. "Have you seen anything strange?"

"Just her," said Corson, jerking her thumb at Nyctasia. They went off together, still arguing.

"Well, if everything's so simple for you here, why don't you do that mirror spell for me? The one I tried to do on the *Windhover*."

"Oh, very well," said Nyctasia, "but I'll wager you'll be disappointed. Fetch your mirror and meet me over there." She pointed to a nearby stand of trees.

Corson had never expected her to agree, and now that Nyctasia was willing, she had her own misgivings. When she went for the mirror she remembered what had befallen those who'd used the spell unwisely, and her apprehensions began to get the better of her.

"Nyc . . . are you sure it's safe to do this? It won't show me something monstrous, will it?"

"I'm glad you take your lessons so much to heart, Corson —you do me credit. No, there's nothing to fear now. The power of this place is free to those within its bounds, if they've the knowledge to wield it. That's what draws magicians here—"

"Like crows to carrion," Corson suggested. "All right, I remember about that. Just get on with it, can't you?"

Nyctasia shook her head indulgently and picked up the mirror, turning it towards Corson.

"Should I close my eyes?" Corson asked anxiously.

"You won't see much if you do. Just think of what you want to see. Leave the rest to me." She calmly recited the spell of Reflection, holding the mirror steadily before Corson's fascinated gaze. The words sounded different from the way Corson remembered them.

At first the mirror showed Corson nothing at all, not even her own features. It was like staring through a window at a colorless winter sky. She tried to think only of Steifann. What would he be doing now? Sleeping, most likely, at this hour—he was always up before daybreak to go to market. But would anyone be sharing his bed?

Suddenly Corson gasped and leaned closer, straining to make out the distant shape barely visible in the glass. In her excitement, she forgot the mirror and her own surroundings. She could not have said whether the hazy images were drawing closer to her, or she to them.

"Ohh," Corson whispered, transfixed.

Steifann was not asleep. He sat at the table in his room with his account books spread before him, carefully sliding the stones back and forth along the wires of a small counting-frame. He was hunched over his work, leaning on one elbow, his hair falling into his eyes. Every so often he glanced longingly at the bed. The candles had burned low. Yawning, he picked up a quill and began to enter figures in the ledger, but then the nib splayed out and left a blot of ink on the page. Steifann threw down the pen in disgust and got to his feet, stretching wearily. He went to the washstand and bent over the basin to splash water in his face, then shook his head briskly. Wiping his face on his sleeve, he returned to his stool and resignedly scraped away at the inkstain with a sharp knife. Steifann prided himself on keeping neat records.

Corson hated to see him so tired. "Steifann, get to bed, leave that for tomorrow. I can go to market with Annin in the morning." Reaching out to touch his shoulder, she struck her hand against the silver mirror, and it was Nyctasia who answered her.

"Come to your senses, Corson, he can't hear you." She laid the mirror face down on the ground.

"Where . . ." cried Corson, looking around in dismay. She snatched at the mirror but it showed her only her own baffled face. "But I . . . he . . ."

"I know," Nyctasia said gently.

"It's—it's a cheat!"

"Yes, in a way. It's a corrupt spell, turned to self-serving ends. It rarely gives what it promises."

Corson was both angry and ashamed—she felt guilty not only for spying on Steifann, but for taking more from him than she ever gave in return. If she were there now, Steifann wouldn't have to work all day and half the night, too.

The wretched mirror spell had revealed her reflection after all, and Corson wasn't pleased with what she saw. "Does magic always make folk feel worse than they did before?" she demanded.

"Usually," said Nyctasia.

The perpetual twilight of the forest made it impossible to tell day from night, and the travelers soon lost all track of time. Even when the sky was visible through the densely laced treetops, it showed a monotonous grey cast that might have been seen at any hour.

There were no definite landmarks, and they seemed always to be riding through the same stretch of wilderness again and again. When they halted to rest, the light from their cooking fire made the surrounding gloom seem even deeper and more forbidding. They spoke in whispers, while the sounds of the forest, usually distant and elusive, drew all too near.

"That's only wolves, that howling," said one of the merchants. "They won't come close to a fire."

"Werewolves, most likely. We should make torches."

"Werewolves don't fear fire," Nyctasia said. "They make fires themselves. In fact, the sort of werewolves that inhabit the Yth only assume human form in order to make fires, or tend wounds—tasks that require hands, you see." She warmed to her subject. "It's also said they prefer to mate that way, though I don't claim to know how that particular information was obtained. For most things they consider the human form inferior to the lupine."

"Then how can you kill them?" someone interrupted.

"Why, just as you'd kill any animal. But they hunt in packs like other wolves. Of course. . . ."

Corson nudged her, and she looked up to meet hostile stares on all sides. Those who had been worried that a were-wolf might spring into their midst were not heartened at the prospect of being attacked by an entire pack. Nyctasia smiled disarmingly. "But of course there's no danger if we stay on the road—nothing in the forest will set foot on it. Just don't let anything tempt you from the road!"

"No fear of that. Nothing could get me into that cursed forest!"

Everyone in the party agreed, but when they next woke,

the guard who had last been on watch was not to be found.

They broke camp hurriedly. "There's no use in our waiting. He won't come back."

"No one ever does."

"That's not so!" said Nyctasia sharply. "Some come back. If you see him by the side of the road, don't listen to him, don't look at him! And for *vahn's* sake, stay out of his reach."

"But how could we be sure?" asked another of the guards, unhappily. "He's my friend."

"If he comes onto the road he's your friend. But don't try to help him. If you were his friend you're in more danger than the rest of us."

"That's true," someone agreed. "You know the song about the enchanted groom."

People nodded. "The Marriage of Makine."

Nyctasia rode up beside the grieving woman. "Do you know the song?"

"No, lady."

"Perhaps you should. It's a pretty song, though a sad one." Her clear voice pierced the eerie silence.

> "There was dancing by the river
>   On the eve of the marriage-tide,
>   Till a calling from the forest
>   Drew the bridegroom from the bride.
>
> "He left his friends, he left the feast,
>   And the dancing in the meadow.
>   He left the one he loved the best
>   To follow a shining shadow.
>
> "She waited all night in the field alone,
>   All night she called his name
>   To guide him back from the forest black,
>   And with the dawn he came.
>
> "She ran and took him in her arms
>   She kissed his eyes that were so wild.
>   'Oh look at me, my love,' said she,
>   And he looked on her and smiled.

" 'Oh speak to me, my love,' she said,
  'This very morn shall we be wed.'
  She kissed his lips that were so cold—
  'I heard you call,' was all he said.

"She led him from the wood away,
  Across the field to the river's edge,
  But he would not ford the rushing stream
  Nor set his foot upon the bridge.

"And then she knew what thing it was
  That came to take her lover's place.
  She saw its image mirrored clear
  Upon the water's face.

"Swiftly o'er the bridge she fled,
  Nor stayed for him that sought her,
  For only those of the living dead
  Will not cross living water.

"It was the calling from the forest
  Drew the bridegroom from the bride.
  And there was never a wedding-fest
  Again at the riverside."

"Bad luck to sing that here, maybe," someone said, after a while.

They rode on in the timeless twilight.

From then on, Nyctasia insisted on staying with Corson whenever she was on guard duty. Corson was secretly glad of the company, but she indignantly denied that she needed Nyctasia's protection.

"Nothing in that forest could be more of a nuisance than you are." Corson took up a stick and raked a potato from under the ashes. She bit off half and wiped her mouth on her sleeve.

"Corson, you have the manners of an ox."

"Mulghfth?" said Corson. She swallowed, and offered the half-eaten potato to Nyctasia. "Did you want some?"

Nyctasia hid her face in her hands and groaned. "You must be joking."

But there was no answer, and she looked up to see Corson staring past her, open-mouthed. Nyctasia turned, and a sickening fear rose within her.

It was just as perilously beautiful as she'd heard. It held out its arms and laughed, and its laughter was sweet, melodic, entrancing.

Burning with a sinister splendor, the Yth-Elf leaned toward them, and its body was a ripple of flame and shadow in the half-light of the forest.

Corson rose to her feet slowly, and the movement roused Nyctasia from her dazed contemplation of the radiant, sensual figure. "Corson!" she cried. "Don't look! Wait!" She tried to pull Corson back, but Corson only thrust her roughly aside and started to move toward the Elf.

Nyctasia seized Corson's pack and hastily spilled out the contents. She found the silver mirror and ran to hold it up before Corson's eyes, frantically chanting a spell:

"Behold in this enchanted mirror
images reversed, but clearer.
Herein all things reveal themselves.
Behold the passion of the Elves!"

Corson backed away, but she could not take her eyes from the glass. Horrorstricken, she dashed the mirror from Nyctasia's hand and fell to her knees, sobbing and retching.

Nyctasia stood over her protectively and dared to look back once at the Elf. It glared at her now, its exquisite features contorted with fury. For a moment she met the creature's challenging gaze before it retreated among the trees. She heard it laugh again—not with seductive sweetness, but in a shrill, mindless titter that seemed to mock her.

"So that's the game is it?" Nyctasia thought, with a certain satisfaction. So be it. She would not be taken unawares.

Corson looked dubiously at the cup of thick, greenish liquid Nyctasia had given her. "It smells disgusting."

"I'm afraid it probably tastes disgusting, too," Nyctasia said apologetically. "Dried herbs wouldn't be as bitter, but there's no apothecary's shop to hand, so fresh ones will have to do. It will give you a dreamless sleep, I promise you."

Corson had not had an easy night's rest since she'd seen the Elf. She lay awake for hours, and when at last she fell asleep she was plagued by terrifying nightmares that left her wakeful again. With a grimace, she shut her eyes and drank down the potion in two gulps. "Hlann's blood, that's foul!"

"I had nothing to sweeten it with. You'll soon sleep, all the same." Nyctasia spread a blanket on the floor of the tent. "Come lie down."

Corson swallowed some water to wash away the taste of the sleeping draught, then threw herself down beside Nyctasia. "I don't feel any sleepier than I did," she complained. "That slime of yours probably won't help at all."

"It will help, if you let it," Nyctasia said patiently. "Just lie quiet. If I had my harp I'd sing you a lullaby."

"You ought to read to me from one of those books of yours. They're dull enough to make anyone sleep."

Nyctasia laughed. "Goodnight, Corson."

"Night!" Corson mumbled. "Who knows whether it's night or day in this Hlann-forsaken forest . . ." She yawned.

Nyctasia watched her for a time. "Corson—"

"Hmm?"

"May I borrow your dagger and leave you mine in its place? I'll bring yours back to you—I swear it on my honor as a Vahnite."

"If you like," said Corson drowsily. It seemed an odd request. Bring it back from where? And there was something else she should ask Nyctasia, but she was so sleepy. . . . For a moment it came to her and she roused herself just long enough to say, "Nyc, where did you find those herbs?"

Nyctasia leaned over her, gently stroking her hair. "Hush, Corson, sleep now. Don't worry."

33

ENTERING THE FOREST was, for Nyctasia, like coming into a
garden after years in a barren wasteland. It was radiant with
life, a wellspring of power. She felt that the world she had
known until now was the domain of death—that she had
escaped from some dire captivity.

She looked back at the road and was overcome with terror.
It looked to her like the ghost of a dead, dried river—a river
of evil that hungered to draw her in and drown her. The very
dust of the road seemed to be the powdered bones of its vic-
tims. Surely, if she set foot upon it, it would leech the life
from her and leave her one of the lost, shadowy creatures who
wandered the road, only fit to be prey for ghouls or the per-
verse Elves. She shuddered, not at the ways of the Yth, but at
the horror of the road—banishment from the source of life.
She turned her eyes away in loathing.

Nyctasia willingly allowed herself to harbor the inhuman
feelings that flooded her. She wished to know the voice of the
Yth in all its treacherous glamour—to resist its lure because
she chose to do so, not because she refused to hear it. To
understand the Yth's power was to master it.

She touched the hilt of Corson's dagger, the token of the
oath that bound her to return. It was a primitive spell, but all
the more powerful for that. She forced herself to look back at
the road, to see it as it was, and she smiled at the sight of it,
familiar and reassuring. It was the way to her true home and
her own kind. Unafraid, she turned and moved off deeper into
the Yth.

The forest was as curious about Nyctasia as she was about it. Leaves brushed her face as she passed, and a grey bird lit on her shoulder and tried to steal one of her silver earrings. But she was not to be caught so easily. She would leave nothing belonging to her within the Yth's power.

All about her there was a furtive rustling that quieted whenever she paused to listen. Even the wind seemed to follow her, whispering, carrying the sound of distant voices.

Nyctasia knelt to study a cluster of pale yellow mushrooms growing at the foot of a hollow tree. She held herself very still and watched from the corner of her eye, hoping that whatever hid nearby would take courage and draw nearer. The thickets stirred with wary, sly movements. She thought a pallid face peered out from the branches of a tree, but it vanished before she could turn to look. There was a frantic scurrying of shadows and Nyctasia was left in an absolute, ominous silence.

She looked up to see that the missing guard from the caravan was approaching her. He moved haltingly and his face was set in a mirthless, tight-lipped smile. He did not speak to her.

Nyctasia had expected this. Rising unhurriedly, she faced him and made a Sign of Command, then uttered a simple spell of Unveiling. He backed away, grinning in rage, and Nyctasia saw that his teeth were sharp and jagged, and slanted back towards his throat.

Then the creature lost all resemblance to the guard. It crouched on its haunches, snarling at Nyctasia, but when she took a step towards it, it turned and swiftly loped away.

Nyctasia meant to find the man, alive or dead, and this creature could lead her to him. She started in pursuit, but it ran faster than a person could follow on foot.

She would not be a person, then. This was the Yth, where one's form only reflected the need of the moment, and her need was for speed and stealth and the keen senses of a hunter. Almost at once, a shape like a small silver fox darted through the trees and took up the chase.

Nyctasia was familiar with the Principle of Transformation. A shifting spell was not intended to change one thing into another, but to manifest the truth that all things were, in essence, one and the same. But only here, with the power of the

Yth at her command, could she avail herself of this knowledge
without risk. The teaching had always seemed to her more of
an ideal than a reality.

Now it seemed altogether natural to take on a different
shape, for this shape belonged to her as well. When it no
longer suited her ends, she would simply discard it for another. She ran effortlessly, keeping track of her quarry by
scent and hearing alone. She was assailed by a myriad of
smells and sounds, some alluring and some threatening, but
she kept to her course unswervingly.

All at once there was a familiar scent on the wind that
made her stop and hug the ground, prowling about and sniffing. She gave a sharp whine. It was the smell of man, the
smell of death. Nyctasia had found what she was seeking.

"Wake up, you! Your friend's gone. Do you know what's
become of her?"

Still muzzy-headed, Corson said vaguely, "Who, Nyc? She
was right here a moment ago."

"She's nowhere in camp, I tell you! Get up, everyone's to
be counted."

It was soon determined that no one was missing except
Nyctasia.

"She's the one who knew all about the forest. If it could get
her, no one is safe!"

"She knew too much about it, if you ask me. I never did
trust that one."

Corson was sure that Nyctasia had left the road by her own
wish, but would she return? She wanted to wait, but the others
insisted on moving the camp. Whatever had taken Nyctasia
might still be close by.

While they took down the tents and harnessed the horses,
Corson paced back and forth along the edge of the road,
shouting for Nyctasia. No one told her to help load the
wagons, but neither did they help her to call. Corson knew
what they were thinking. She was thinking the same thing—
what if Nyctasia *did* come back . . . ?

Nyctasia was walking beside a stream, gathering some
sweet-smelling herbs, when she heard Corson's voice calling.
She paid no heed to it at first but kept on her way, following

the stream until she found that it was leading her back to camp. Surely not so soon? She stopped and sat down beside a shallow pool, trying to sort out her thoughts.

She dipped her hand in the clear water, and silvery minnows swam into her palm, curious and unafraid. Her reflection rippled as though with laughter. Gazing down at it, Nyctasia hardly knew its features for her own.

"Images reversed but clearer," she murmured. Why should she renounce the power and freedom of the Yth for the sake of that stranger mirrored in the pool? What would she lose by yielding to the fascination of the forest?

Corson's voice pulled at her like an answer to her questions, but she set her back to it and struck off aimlessly through the forest. She wandered among the whispering leaves and beckoning shadows, wishing to lose herself in the depths of the Yth, but still she could hear Corson calling her. Whichever way she turned, the shouting only grew louder, and she was soon within sight of the road again. Resigned, Nyctasia drew nearer to the campsite until she stood almost at the edge of the road. Half-hidden by the thickly tangled bushes, she watched the caravan prepare to depart. They were almost ready. She must have been gone longer than she'd intended.

Corson was no longer shouting. She stood in the middle of the road, looking about her hopelessly. Someone came over to her, and Nyctasia could hear them arguing, then Corson shrugged and followed after him.

Nyctasia approached reluctantly. Try as she might, she could not let her promise go unfulfilled.

"Wait!" She came to the edge of the road and held the dagger out to Corson.

For a moment, everyone was frightened into silence, then people shouted to Corson to keep her place.

Corson needed no warning. She made no move towards Nyctasia, but only drew her sword and waited, her face cold as stone.

Their fear amused Nyctasia. And Corson seemed most laughable of all, brandishing a sword as if such a weapon could avail against the Yth's magic. She could destroy the lot of them if she chose!

"Corson, come away! Leave her!" the drivers whipped up

the cart horses, and folk scrambled to mount the wagons, calling to each other to hurry. Corson began to back away, never taking her eyes from Nyctasia. Drawn against her will out of the shelter of the forest, Nyctasia followed her, still proffering the dagger.

Seeing her walk onto the road, Corson allowed her to approach. "Nyc . . . ?"

"I told you I'd bring it back. You needn't have worried."

Corson's relief was overmastered by rage. Seizing Nyctasia by the collar, she shook her roughly and shouted, "If you ever try a fool's trick like that again, you'll wish you'd been keel-hauled before I finish with you!"

Nyctasia let herself be railed at and buffeted about, without a word of protest. When Corson paused for breath, she merely straightened her clothes and said mildly, "It is written, 'If the Yth fails to make you its prey, beware lest it make you a predator.' You're quite right, Corson, I shouldn't have gone. I'm sorry."

"You are?!"

"Yes, I was wrong. It was far more dangerous than I expected."

Corson was dumbfounded. Nothing she had anticipated was as unsettling as winning an argument with Nyctasia.

"It takes a witch to enter the Yth and return, so be thankful you have a witch with you!" Nyctasia said defiantly. "If I hadn't gone *she* would have, and we'd have lost her as well." She pointed at one of the guards. "You've seen him, haven't you?"

The woman nodded. "He wouldn't speak to me," she said softly.

"We wouldn't let her go to him. She wanted to," one of the others volunteered.

"I thought as much. Listen to me, I found him—he's dead, you must understand that. Here, I brought you this as proof." Nyctasia handed her a brass armlet. "I don't think you'll see him again."

"Thank you, lady," the woman sobbed.

"Now, if you're all satisfied, I should like to get some rest," Nyctasia said scornfully.

No one answered her, but when she was out of earshot

someone muttered, "We ought to kill that one, if you ask me."

"No one's asked you!" Corson snapped, loud enough for the rest to hear. "If anyone's to kill her, it'll be me. I've earned the pleasure!"

34

Nyctasia had put on her new suit of black velvet for the first time that morning, and she looked more the lady than Corson had ever seen her.

But Corson was haggard and worn, and she didn't even try to conceal it. "What are you waiting for?" she asked Nyctasia impatiently.

Nyctasia had reined in her horse at the crossroads and was letting the rest of the party pass her by. "I'm not going into Hlasven itself. The other road leads closer to my way."

"You go where you like. I want to spend the night at the inn. I'm tired, Nyc."

"I know. You'll find a bed sooner if you come with me. We're closer to 'Ben's home now than to the hostel."

Corson turned her horse. "All right then. I'd like to see if he's as beautiful as you say."

Nyctasia took the lead. The road gradually gave way to an overgrown track which branched and meandered, sometimes disappearing completely—but Nyctasia never hesitated. She rode through pathless fields and stretches of dense woods as confidently as if the way were clearly marked before her.

"You must have been here before!" Corson accused. "You know the way too well."

"'Ben gave me very careful directions. I've studied them so often, I know them by rote."

"That won't do." Corson halted her horse. "I know you think me a fool, but even a fool knows that no one could travel so surely through land unknown to them—not even with a good map in hand. You've lied to me all along." She did not sound angry, only resigned and weary.

"Corson, no . . . I'm sorry . . . I didn't think you'd care to hear the truth. I've not been here before but I don't have to look for the way because the way is looking for me."

"You're right, I don't want to hear this. I'd rather you were just lying. How much farther is it, can you tell?"

"We're close, Corson, I feel it!" She laughed excitedly. "Close to home!"

Soon the path reappeared and widened to a broad track that led through cleared ground. Nyctasia suddenly spurred her horse to a gallop.

Corson followed more slowly. Far ahead of her, she saw Nyctasia race to meet another rider. He lifted Nyctasia onto his own horse and, to Corson, they seemed to become one figure.

As she approached them, he was saying, "'Tasia, how could you cut off your hair? You look like a street urchin." He held the reins with one arm and Nyctasia with the other.

"Or a vagabond student?" suggested Nyctasia. "But perhaps I'll let it grow again, now."

Corson had never seen her so carefree and elated. "She's beautiful," Corson realized, trying unsuccessfully to picture Nyctasia with long hair.

Watching them, Corson had to admit that for once Nyctasia had been telling the truth when she'd boasted of her handsome lover. He was all she'd claimed—lean and graceful, with a tense, whiplike frame that suggested carefully controlled power. Intense blue eyes burned against his dark skin, and thick black hair framed the sculpted planes of his face. Corson could well understand Nyctasia's passion for him.

"And this is Corson," Nyctasia was saying. "I'd never have reached the coast alive without her."

Lord Erystalben looked at Corson for the first time. "Then she is welcome," he said. Without waiting for a reply, he wheeled his horse about and rode ahead, leaving Corson to follow with Nyctasia's mount. She had only to ride straight before her, for the walls of the keep could now be seen in the distance.

Corson was not offended by his treatment of her. He and

Nyctasia had been parted for so long—how should he spare a thought for anyone else? And in truth, it was a relief to be spared further courtesies when all she wanted to do was rest.

She was met at the gates by a groom who took charge of the horses, while another servant offered to show her to her quarters. Corson gratefully followed.

Even when she found herself assigned to cramped servants' quarters, Corson made no objection. She fell onto the narrow bed and was asleep at once.

* * *

Corson woke suddenly, confused, and for a sickening moment thought that she was still in the forest. Yet even as she realized where she was, the feeling persisted, like a dream she could neither quite remember nor quite forget. She would not have admitted to being frightened, but she rose at once and went in search of company.

Everyone fell silent as she entered the kitchen.

"Good day to all. My name's Corson."

No one offered a name in return. Finally, one of the women said, "You'll have something to eat? Some ham and dripping-bread?"

Corson remembered that it was said to be unwise to speak one's name in an enchanted place—or to eat or drink anything offered. She'd never put much faith in such tales, but she found that she had no appetite now. "No, I thank you. Let someone tell the Lady Nyctasia that I want to see her."

"She's with His Lordship."

"I don't care if she's with all the gentry of the Maritime Alliance—she'll see me! Take me to her!"

But they paid no attention to her demands. The woman went back to rendering ham fat in a pan. Scullions continued their scrubbing, and cleared ashes from the hearth.

"If you're sent for, you'll be told," said a man whom Corson took for the steward.

That Lord Erystalben should think her a lackey was understandable, but why had Nyctasia sent her no word? She glared at Shiastred's people, whose very calmness was unnerving. "Are you folk of flesh and blood, or of sand and smoke and spells?! This place reeks of magic. I'm leaving! Tell Her Ladyship I'd better things to do than wait on her pleasure. Tell her I've gone, if she thinks to ask!"

The steward rose. "You are free to go. We've no orders to hold you here. I'll have your horse brought. Follow me."

Corson lost most of that afternoon searching for the elusive path that led back to the road, and it was late in the day before she came upon familiar landmarks. Knowing that she would lose her way again if she traveled by night, she resigned herself to sleeping in the open.

As daylight faded, she made a tidy pile of dry twigs and bark for a fire. Flint and steel were in her pack, and she soon coaxed the spark into a small but comforting blaze that allayed her solitude. If she set out at first light, she could reach the crossroads by noon. Soon she would be on the great trunk road that skirted the Yth and led back towards Mehomne. She was going home—and with enough money in her pockets to set the folk at Steifann's back on their heels.

Corson stared into the fire, wondering, not for the first time, if the real reason she continued in her restless, wandering ways was the pleasure she took in coming home to the Hare. She always reveled in the commotion she caused when she arrived, unlooked for, loaded with gifts and full of wild, exaggerated tales about her daring exploits. Naturally, no one believed these stories—except for the cook's children, who could never hear enough of her adventures. They'd run about waving wooden swords, playing at warriors, until Walden threatened to use Corson for stew-meat if she didn't stop filling their heads with her rubbish.

But after the excitement of her homecoming had waned, Corson would soon begin to tire of the familiar pattern of life at the Hare. There was plenty of work to be done, and Corson did her share, but she could never get used to the monotony of doing the same chores day after day.

Steifann always gave her a hearty welcome and urged her to stay, but his time was largely taken up with the responsibilities of keeping the tavern. He never seemed to tire of the endless round of marketing and cooking, overseeing both the help and the customers, and studying his account books. Despite his generosity and good humor, Steifann was known as a shrewd man of business, and the tavern turned a tidy profit under his direction.

"You're a slave to this place!" Corson had once complained. "You won't even come on a fortnight's journey with me. What good's all this to you, if you're just a drudge?"

"At least I know where my next meal's coming from, which is more than you do—except when you're cadging from me!" Though Corson earned her way at the Hare, Steifann always joked that she ate enough for three. "I'll probably end my days in the alms-house from feeding you."

Corson tugged playfully at his beard. "I do well enough on my own."

"So does a stray dog, but that doesn't mean that you should live like an animal. And die like an animal," he added soberly. "You've never had a home, Corson, but if you live long enough to learn common sense you'll be glad of a roof over your head."

"And just remember," he teased, "if you don't choose to settle down with me, there are others who'd be glad of the chance—"

He got no further because Corson gave a yell of outrage and shoved him out of the bed, which put an end to the argument for then.

Though Corson's carping about Steifann's other bedmates was mostly in jest, she did worry that he might find someone else better suited to his way of life. When the boredom of chopping wood and peeling vegetables grew too great, she sometimes hired on with the city guard of Chiastelm just to be near him, but her days in the army had left her with little taste for routine and regimentation. Anything that curbed her freedom felt like a trap to Corson, even Steifann's concern for her.

Still, looking back over her bleak and brutal past, she could see that what Steifann offered her was better by far than any life she had yet known. In the army, she'd only been marking time until the moment when a sword or spear would make her food for the crows. When she was forced to fight, she fought with ferocity and cunning; she ate whatever was doled out to her, then stole from those weaker than herself; and, hardest of all, she learned to obey her superiors' orders well enough to avoid being beaten into the dirt.

When her term in the army was over, Corson had set out on her own, determined to live as she liked and let nothing hinder her. She went wherever a skilled sword was needed, traveling from place to place, squandering her pay on gambling and ale. Her newfound freedom often brought her nights in prison, where she lay sick with drink until the magistrates saw fit to release her—taking whatever money she might have left. It was only through good fortune that Corson had so far escaped the early death that was the common fate of her kind.

Her first piece of luck was Desmalkin, a young student, who was thrown into her cell one night for trying to cheat an innkeeper. They'd taken up with each other for a few months, and his company had been a civilizing influence on Corson. She was in awe of his sophistication and learning, and he was gratified by her obvious admiration. She had insisted that he teach her to read, more to gain his respect than from a desire to better herself. But 'Malkin was pleased with her progress, and even Corson began to suspect that there might be more to life than mere survival.

'Malkin had his own ambitions, however, and when he entered the service of a provincial nobleman as a scribe, he found that it no longer suited his position to be seen with a common ruffian like Corson. She was hurt and bitter, and before long had fallen back into her old habits.

Corson's second piece of luck had been Steifann. Unlike the polished 'Malkin, he genuinely cared for Corson, but he couldn't afford to harbor troublemakers at the Hare and he would make no exceptions for her. Time and again, Corson would ride off, swearing never to return. She would be again as she had been, free, with no thought for anyone but herself.

But wherever she went she found herself thinking, "What would Steifann say to this?" and "Wait till Steifann hears about that!"—and in time she'd find a reason to return to Chiastelm. Steifann's hold on her was frightening, but Corson wasn't sure she wanted to break free. Often, while he slept, she would study his face as though its features held the answer to a question she had not yet learned to ask. Had all her traveling been in search of that answer—and had she now found it only to lose it again through her own blindness? Was her vaunted freedom really no more than aimlessness and license?

Corson picked up a twig and began to strip off bits of bark. "After all, what freedom do I really have? Always following someone else's orders—'Very good, my lord . . . Yes, my lady . . .' bowing and scraping and maybe dying for some nasty little aristocrat who can't even be bothered to bid me farewell—!" She snapped the twig in two and tossed it into the fire. "Steifann's worth the lot of them!"

The vision conjured up by the mirror spell continued to haunt her. She should be in Chiastelm with Steifann, not traipsing about like a tinker! Why couldn't she make up her mind to stay with him, then?

If her life had been crueler before she met Steifann, at least it had been simpler, Corson thought ruefully. In those days she had been all of a piece—she had acted without hesitation and suffered no afterthoughts. But now there seemed to be two Corsons, each clamoring for something different. One wanted the affection and security that Steifann could give her, while the other still feared confinement more than loneliness, still drew her strength from a black pool of hatred and anger. Would that demon never let her rest?

Corson yawned and moved closer to the fire. The night was turning cooler and a light breeze had come up. "What's the good of maundering on like this?" she chided herself. "I'm just tired and hungry, that's what ails me." She made a poor meal on the remains of the provisions in her saddlebag, and wished that she'd accepted the offer of food from Shiastred's cook. Now that she was well away from the place her qualms seemed like foolishness, and the sense of shadowy menace had left her. Sighing, Corson stood and began to scuff out the fire, then lay down and shifted about, trying to find a softer spot of ground. "Asye, but I must be getting old. Time was when I'd sleep in the mud for weeks and not give it a thought."

Overhead, the stars burned clear as candles in the cloudless night sky. "A fair day tomorrow and good traveling." Corson pulled the saddle blanket over her shoulders and slept soundly until dawn, undisturbed by sinister dreams.

35

A DAY'S EASY ride brought her to the roadside hostel. A meal
and some strong ale was what she needed now.

A few of her fellow travelers from the merchant troupe
were sitting together at supper, but when Corson greeted them
she was met with a hostile silence. Bewildered, she turned to
one of the guards who'd stood watch with her. "What's the
matter here?"

He gestured toward a corner table where someone sat
slumped over a tankard of ale. "Everyone knows you're her
friend. I'd get her out of here if I were you," he said, and
turned his back on Corson.

"Oh no," said Corson. "It can't be!" But there was nothing
for it. She crossed the room to Nyctasia's table.

"Corson! How delightful! Will you have a drink?" She
leaned back in her chair and waved for more ale. "Did I ever
tell you that your name is a corrupt form of 'Corisonde'? At
least I think it is."

"You're drunk!"

"I looked for you when I left, but you'd already gone—
and very sensible of you, too. I thought I'd pass you on the
way here."

"I lost my way. What are you doing here? Where's Lord
Collarbone?"

Nyctasia looked at her dully. "'Ben? He's—he's dead, I
think. . . . I don't know." She shuddered and took a long
draught of her ale.

Corson sat down. "What are you talking about?"

For a moment, Nyctasia's eyes held a terrible clarity. "Everything that is taken must be paid for," she said. "But there are ways of making others pay for what one takes. The *vahn* forbids such a thing. . . . I can never return to him now, I must not!" Staring into her empty tankard, she said softly, "I might better have stayed in Rhostshyl to be murdered, what does it matter?" She began to rock back and forth, her face in her hands. "Kastenid tried to warn me, but how could I believe him? I want more ale."

"You've had your fill. You're not used to drink."

Nyctasia laughed wildly. "That's because I never knew it was such an effective Consolation!" She seemed to find this extraordinarily funny. She reached for Corson's tankard and, as Corson snatched it from her, she tossed a gold coin into the ale. "Look!" she said proudly. A goldfish was swimming in the dark liquor.

Corson gasped and dropped the tankard. Ale spattered their boots, and the coin rolled across the floor. No one picked it up. "Nyctasia," Corson said tensely, "a lady does not make a spectacle of herself in public!"

Nyctasia giggled. "So beware, my Lady Alys," she sang tipsily. She threw back her head and drew a deep breath, then let it out slowly with a look of intense concentration. To Corson's horror, three large, pale moths drifted from Nyctasia's mouth, one after another. They fluttered about erratically then dissolved in the air like smoke.

"That tickles," Nyctasia remarked, laughing.

Corson now understood the suspicion that surrounded them. Those who lived near the forest mistrusted magic, and the travelers had been wary of Nyctasia from the start. They took her for some creature of the Yth—and Corson was not quite sure that they were wrong.

Nyctasia had begun to trace patterns on the tabletop with the spilled ale, muttering to herself in some foreign tongue. "I think I'll summon a demon," she announced loudly, raising one arm in a dramatic gesture. A serving-girl shrieked and dashed for the kitchen. Several people started to their feet, seizing knives or staffs. A heavy earthenware pot struck Nyctasia's shoulder.

Corson grabbed her by the wrist and dragged her to the door. They were both thrust roughly into the yard amidst shouted threats and curses. Someone threw Nyctasia's satchel of books out after them, and the door was slammed and bolted.

Nyctasia sat up and tried to wipe the mud from her face with an equally muddy hand. "I'm an Edonaris," she protested, slurring her words slightly, "and a Rhaicime! How dare they!"

Corson kicked her. "Get up, *lady*," she spat. "Rhaicime! Rutting half-wit! You almost got our throats cut for us!"

Nyctasia rose unsteadily to her feet and regarded Corson with wounded dignity. "You are forthwith dismissed from my service. Leave me!"

"I ought to! I don't know what stops me—I must be bewitched. Come along!" She led Nyctasia to the stables and heaved her, none too gently, onto her horse.

Even drunk, Nyctasia instinctively gripped with her knees to keep her seat. "Where are we going, love?" she asked amiably, following Corson out of the courtyard.

"There's a village about a league down the Hlasven road. We'll find some sort of shelter there." Corson thought resentfully of the lost comforts at the hostel. "I didn't even get a meal. You and your stinking sorcery! Moths . . . ! It's disgusting!"

"I don't think I could really summon a demon," Nyctasia said wistfully. "Of course I've never tried it so close to the Yth."

Corson rode closer to her and took her roughly by the arm. "You're not about to try it now, either—I'll break your arm first!"

Nyctasia smiled blandly at her. "Yes, Maeg."

"Asye . . . !" sighed Corson, and rode ahead. They went on in silence broken only by snatches of songs and spells from Nyctasia.

> "Behold in this enchanted mirror
> images reversed but clearer.
> Patterns of shattered shadow yield
> their mysteries in silverglass revealed.
> Read if you will the gleaming's meaning,
> Pierce the . . . something . . . mmm . . . seeming.
> Deep in. . . ."

"I forget the rest," she yawned.

"Good. I don't want to hear that. Sing something else."

" 'The Cold Ballad'?" suggested Nyctasia.

> "And some folk said that she had died
> Through working of a curse.
> A doll, a needle in its side,
> An image shrouded in a band?
> And others whispered worse.
> Had she not enemies in the land?
> Forbidden rivalry, bitter scorn—
> They guessed at poison in her wine,
> A venom'd thorn,
> A length of twine,
> A sudden, smothering hand?

> "But no one ever shall discover,
> Nor guess, what she walked out to find.
> A rose, a shell, her demon lover
> Perhaps her peace of mind . . ."

Nyctasia stopped abruptly.

"Is that the end?"

"No, there's another verse, but I've never understood it. I don't even like that song," she said petulantly.

"Oh, hold your noise. There's someone coming. We must be near the village." Peering into the darkness, Corson could make out two figures approaching on foot, one holding up a lantern. "We can ask them about lodgings."

"You there—" she called, but the man in front went straight to Nyctasia and took the reins of her horse.

" 'Ben!" she exclaimed happily, leaning over to caress his cheek, "I've missed you terribly. . ." She reached down to him and he caught her by the waist and lifted her from the saddle. "I can't walk," she laughed.

"No matter, 'Tasia, we've not far to go. I'll carry you." He picked her up easily, cradling her in his arms, and started back along the dark road.

Corson dismounted hastily. "My lord, where are you taking her? Wait!" Shiastred's servant laid a warning hand on her arm, but she shook him off and followed. Nyctasia had not

made much sense that evening, but she had certainly meant to
break with Lord Erystalben. Corson stepped in front of him,
barring the way.

"Stand aside," he commanded. Nyctasia looked on curiously, her head nestled against his throat.

"Let her be, she's out of her senses with drink. I can't let
you take her off—"

Shiastred laughed. "Your sense of duty does you credit,
woman, but I assure you, your mistress is not in danger. I
have told you once to stand aside."

"She's not my mistress, and I've told you once to let her
go!" But as Corson stepped towards him, she was stricken
with a sudden irresistible weakness that left her helpless.
Overcome by dizziness, she fell to her knees at Shiastred's
feet. Raising her head with an effort she met his cold blue
eyes, narrowed in anger.

"Call off your watchdog, 'Tasia. She's liable to bite someone."

Puzzled, Nyctasia looked down at Corson crouched in the
road, her face mad with rage and hatred. "Not a watchdog, a
wildcat," Nyctasia said solemnly. "Killed three of my best
hunting dogs." She laid her head back on his shoulder and
closed her eyes, sighing deeply.

"See to her," Shiastred ordered his man, nodding towards
Corson. He walked past her indifferently, bearing Nyctasia off
into the darkness.

"The weakness will pass soon," the servant said. He helped
Corson to rise and mount, then led away Nyctasia's horse.
Corson could only follow.

She asked no questions, and did not look up until they
halted in the yard of a great stone hall. "But where are we?"
She knew of no manor house this side of the village.

"Why, at my lord's holding, of course. He never goes far
hence."

Corson recognized the place now, and her senses reeled in
protest. "But I took the Hlasven road," she cried. "I know I
did!"

36

THE CHAMBER HAD been arranged entirely to Nyctasia's taste, as only one who knew her well could have done it. The furnishings were sparse but rare, of marble and oak and ivory. In the center of the carpet there stood a round table of petrified wood, and the bed filled a niche draped with curtains of dark brocade, shot with silver threads. A mirror in a silver frame hung on one wall, flanked by brackets holding silver candlesticks.

The deeply arched window overlooked a pool amid overgrown gardens, and on the windowseat stood a small, silver-stringed harp of black ebonwood. Shiastred set it aside and laid Nyctasia, half-asleep, among the cushions.

Not until he had left her did she open her eyes and try to sit upright. Her head ached cruelly, and the sight of the chamber sobered her still more, as she began to remember her reasons for leaving it the day before. She took up the black harp and very lightly brushed the strings, but set it down again when she heard Shiastred's footsteps in the corridor.

He handed her a heavy goblet of a steaming, fragrant liquid which she accepted gratefully, knowing that it would ease the throbbing pain behind her eyes.

"And since when have you taken to drink?" he asked.

Nyctasia looked at him over the rim of the goblet. "Since when have you taken to human sacrifice, 'Ben?"

"Don't talk nonsense, 'Tasia! You too have destroyed your enemies—"

"To protect myself, not to increase my own power!"

"Which of them would not do as much to me if they could?" he demanded angrily, but then said more gently, "Sometimes that is the only way to protect oneself. You do not yet know the Yth as I do."

Nyctasia shook her head, still too tipsy to argue. She knew there were reasons, but it was so hard to arrange her thoughts. "I don't care what you do to your enemies, 'Ben. I care what you do to your own spirit."

Shiastred stood over her, as if undecided whether to stay or go, but now he sat at her side, looking out over the dark gardens. "Are you so changed to me 'Tasia? I would not have believed that you could mistrust me, turn from me.... To what end have I won this safehold if not for you––that we might be together, beyond the reach of any enemy?"

"It is not I who have changed. We never thought to pay such a price for our freedom."

"We were children then! Yth-land is not won for the asking, or held by the weak. Kastenid lost this place because he would not do all in his power to keep it. But together we would be proof against any challenge. We'd have no need to use our enemies' ways to defend ourselves. That is what we wanted!"

He drew her into his arms, caressingly massaged her aching temples with strong, knowing fingers. "But if you would renounce our plans now, 'Tasia, we shall leave here together. Let Kastenid take back his own––what can it mean to me if you no longer want it? We will travel if you wish. Only tell me what you want me to do!"

Nyctasia closed her eyes. "I want you to hold me, 'Ben." She knew that she was vulnerable, in her confusion, to Influences she should resist, and that lovemaking would only weaken her further. She knew that there were questions to be asked, plans and promises to be made. Yet she told herself that they would wait, that her desire would not. A chill went through her as Erystalben lightly kissed the back of her neck. "I want you to hold me," she said.

* * *

Corson was awakened next morning by a servant who informed her that she was wanted by Her Ladyship and must come at once.

She had not spent a peaceful night. Too weak to seek other shelter, she'd had no choice but to remain under Shiastred's roof. The sickening dizziness had gradually left her, but sleep had not brought her rest. In her dreams, she was harried by a great hawk that circled about her, raking at her with its talons. Each time she tried to strike down the raptor it swept out of reach of her sword, letting her wear herself out with useless blows, biding its time to strike. She woke still exhausted from the losing battle.

She was suspicious of the summons. Suppose it were a trap? She knew she was at Shiastred's mercy as long as she was within his walls, but how could she get away if every road only led her back to this cursed place? The sense of confinement struck her with a cold panic terror. All her prowess would be unavailing against Shiastred's sorcery. Would she really be allowed to see Nyctasia?

She followed the servant up a long staircase and through a series of winding corridors. He left her at the curtained doorway of Nyctasia's chamber.

"Good morning, Corson. I trust you've been well looked after?" Nyctasia said graciously. She was sitting in bed, wrapped in a robe of silver-grey watered silk.

At first Corson was dumbfounded by Nyctasia's distant manner, but then she saw Lord Erystalben watching them from the alcove window.

Corson stiffened. "I want to talk to you alone."

"Do you hear, 'Ben?" laughed Nyctasia. "You are dismissed!"

He shook his head, smiling tolerantly. "You were always too familiar with your servants, 'Tasia."

"Oh, but one must allow for some spirit. One doesn't want a bodyguard with the gentle temper of a ewe-lamb."

He came to Nyctasia and, leaning over her, lovingly raised her head. "You've no need of a bodyguard now." Pulling her close, he gave her a lingering kiss. Corson moved well out of his way as he went to the door, but he passed her as though she weren't there.

"You've changed your mind again?" Corson asked, feeling like a fool. She sat down on the bed by Nyctasia, uninvited. "When I found you at the hostel you said you would never come back here."

"I'm afraid I don't remember much of what I said last night," Nyctasia admitted ruefully. "I ought not to drink. 'Ben had insisted that we make a marriage pact, and we quarreled —but as you can see, I gave way in the end." She held out her hand to show Corson the slender golden band.

"But what of you, Corson? I thought you were eager to return to Chiastelm." She pointed to a well-filled purse on the table at her bedside. "That will more than meet your needs, though of course you are welcome to stay. You will always be welcome here. I know what I owe you."

Corson did not dare to slap her. "You owe me nothing, lady," she said, rising. "I want to reach the crossroads before dark—have I your leave to go?"

"Of course. A safe journey to you, Corson." She summoned a servant to show Corson out.

37

THIS TIME, CORSON had no difficulty finding her way to the hostel. "If that Yth-taken friend of yours—" the host began.

"She's not with me! And she's not my friend. I want a room!" Corson looked around defiantly, daring anyone to try and put her out. Today she'd give them a fight, and welcome. But no one challenged her, and she was shown at once to a small bedchamber. She ordered some ale and dropped wearily onto a bench by the window overlooking the moonlit roadway.

Corson knew that no one at the inn wanted anything to do with her, and she could hardly blame them. "That ungrateful bitch!" she thought, leaning her arms on the windowsill and staring out into the night. She cursed the day she'd met Nyctasia, she cursed all magicians and then all the aristocracy for good measure. On an angry impulse, she took off the earrings Nyctasia had given her and pushed them into her pouch. "I'll sell the filthy things. I don't want her cast-off trinkets."

"Gold doesn't suit me," she said prissily, mimicking Nyctasia's high voice and aristocratic accent. "Gold's not good enough for her!"

Corson frowned. Some notion seemed to leap out at her like a startled fox, plain in the moonlight for only a moment, then scuttling back into the shadows. Lost in thought, she didn't hear the hesitant knock at the door, and she was startled when the serving-maid appeared with her ale. The girl approached timorously and set a pitcher and mug on the bench next to her. "I don't have any demons in my pockets!" Corson snapped, and the child hurried off in confusion.

"I might as well be a leper, thanks to Her Ladyship!"

Corson shook her head, still vexed by the memory of Nyctasia's indifference. She knew what an accomplished actress Nyctasia could be, but she could not persuade herself that Nyctasia's familiarity with her had all been feigned. If Nyctasia were really as haughty and proud as all that, she would never have taken so much trouble to nurse Corson back to health. She'd have thought it beneath her to cosset and humor a lowly servant like Corson, to wait on her with her own hands.

Had she been acting when she'd dismissed Corson with cold formality? Why should she perform such a masquerade for Corson's benefit—was she afraid of Lord Erystalbcn?

Corson downed a mug of ale and poured herself another. No, Nyctasia had been more than willing to throw in her lot with that bloodless, spindle-shanked bastard, of that Corson was certain. She slammed her fist down on the windowsill. If only there were some way to settle her score with Shiastred! He'd called her a dog, and she'd slunk off like a whipped dog, too. If she could just fight him on her own terms—! She gulped down the last of her ale and went downstairs for more. Though no one was likely to drink with her, she preferred the busy taproom to her own chamber just then. She fetched a fresh pitcher and took a seat at an empty table.

To her surprise, someone did sit down across from her before long. She looked up from her drink. "You again! Let me be—Lady Nyctasia's not here."

"So I see," said Vhar Kastenid. "Where is she?"

Corson took a long pull at her ale. "She's dead."

"Dead—how? What do you mean?"

"You ought to know what it means. She said you were right about him—that he was dead. I wish he was!"

"Then she has left him?" he asked eagerly.

"Well, she did, but she went back again. Of course, she was sotted," Corson snickered.

"Impossible—Lady Nyctasia observes the Discipline. You'd best tell me everything from the beginning."

Corson fell silent. Her wounded pride rankled too keenly for her to tell of her humiliation at Shiastred's hands. "It's none of your affair."

"You don't understand. She's in grave danger."

"She's always in danger!" Corson exploded. "What's it to me? I don't care what becomes of that high-handed, treacherous vixen!"

"But I care what becomes of her, and I need your help. You want vengeance on Shiastred. Don't deny it. This is no time for your cursed sullenness!"

Corson started to her feet, fists clenched. "You—!" But at a look from Kastenid she suddenly caught her tongue. Shiastred had looked at her in that way.

"Sit down," he said quietly.

Corson obeyed. "You're no better than he is," she muttered.

"That's as may be. We want the same things, he and I, but I perhaps am more particular as to how I get them."

"What do you want with me?"

"What would I want with a mercenary but to buy her services? And I pay well." He studied Corson for a long moment. "What is it you fear?"

"I'm no coward!" Corson hesitated, toying with her empty mug. "But I'm . . . helpless. I can't fight Shiastred."

"I don't want you to fight him. That is for me to do. But I cannot challenge him at the source of his power. If he's drawn off his own ground he'll be weaker, and with Lady Nyctasia's help I could defeat him."

"Are you mad? She won't turn against him!"

"I believe she will, once she's freed from his Influence. When she broke the Discipline she abandoned her defenses, and now she's beyond my reach, within his domain. But you can go there freely. She trusts you, and Shiastred has no reason to harm you. He'll not consider you a threat."

"I know. I'm beneath his notice."

He leaned closer to her. "Do you dare to return there?"

It was a wise choice of words to put Corson on her mettle. "I've daring enough. But I warn you, for such a deed I command a noble fee." She did not much trust Kastenid, but without a magician's help she could never hope to foil Lord Erystalben. It could do no harm to hear him out. As he talked, she reached absently into her pouch for the gold earrings and put them on.

*   *   *

"Come for a ride with me," said Corson. "I want to talk to you."

Nyctasia was more than ever a stranger to her. She treated Corson as a favorite, whose familiarity was to be indulged. Shiastred simply took no heed of her—how Nyctasia managed her servants was her own affair.

They rode along a path that led up into the hills toward the stone hut where Kastenid was waiting. "Bring her as far as you can," he'd told Corson. "I'll try to create an Influence to draw her on, but I can do nothing while she remains within his walls."

Nyctasia reined in her horse, frowning. "We've come far enough, Corson. What have you to say to me?"

Corson dismounted. She seated herself on a fallen log and waited for Nyctasia to join her. "I've been with Kastenid, Nyc. He says you're spellcast and I believe it. You're not the same."

"One behaves more freely on the road, of course—formalities may be put aside. But the journey is over now." She looked off into the hills. "So Kastenid hopes to use you to sway me? He is wrong to bring you into this. You do not understand the risks you run."

"I don't trust any magician. Never mind Kastenid—you should come away from here for your own sake. This place is a prison!"

Nyctasia rose. "This is where I belong. Go back to Chiastelm, Corson, you can do no good here." She held out her hand. "Farewell."

Corson shrugged. "I've done my best." She suddenly smiled and reached her right hand out to meet Nyctasia's. "Farewell, Nyc." Her fist caught Nyctasia neatly under the jaw in a swift, stunning blow.

38

"How do you, Lady Nyctasia?" Kastenid asked worriedly, holding a skin of water to her lips. "Can you rise?"

Nyctasia gingerly touched her sore jaw and winced. "I trust you enjoyed doing that," she said to Corson.

"Oh, I did. It was a great pleasure."

"She's been wanting to hit me for a long time," Nyctasia said, turning to Kastenid, "but I do not see what you hope to gain from this. I have answered you for the last time. If you cannot stand against him, you must fall!"

Kastenid was silent, shaken by Nyctasia's unlooked-for scorn. Wearily, he passed his hand over his face and sighed, "at every turn you elude me, lady."

"I'll not be bait to lure him from his stronghold." She went to the doorway of the hut, only pausing to say, "And if you're wise, you'll be gone from here before he takes up your challenge."

"Shall I hit her again?" Corson suggested.

Kastenid looked blindly after Nyctasia. "You were right," he said finally, "she is dead."

But a moment later they heard Nyctasia's high, clear laughter outside. "No, it was my own fault," she said. "Come away."

"Shiastred! You'll deal with me first!" Kastenid shouted. Corson reluctantly followed him outside.

"Just as you will," said Erystalben ar'n Shiastred, smiling. "I should have dealt with you long ago." He was perfectly confident and at his ease.

174

"'Ben, there's no need for this," Nyctasia urged. "He can be no threat to us now."

"It is not I who insist upon it. I've spared you once before, Kastenid. I shall do so again if you let me."

Kastenid, too, smiled. "I'll not find you so far from your lair again."

Shiastred gestured in resignation. "Speak to him, 'Tasia. Perhaps he'll listen to you."

"Come to your senses, Kastenid. You seek your own destruction."

He barely glanced at her. "If you will not stand with me, stand aside."

"Enough!" said Shiastred, and suddenly they were surrounded by an intense silence. Corson could not tell when the conflict had begun. Neither man moved—they still stood facing one another across the stony ground, but they no longer smiled. No leaf stirred and the air grew still and heavy. But Corson remembered how Shiastred had struck her down on the road without a blow, and nothing could have made her walk between the two magicians.

Nyctasia was white and rigid with tension. She never took her eyes from Shiastred, and when he reached out to her she went to his side at once. Kastenid staggered suddenly and fell back a pace.

"Nyc, don't!" Corson gasped, hardly knowing what she meant. Nyctasia turned to her, and Corson was certain that for a moment her grey eyes were a vivid blue.

"Don't interfere in this, Corson. I have no quarrel with you." She raised her hand in warning, and Corson suddenly saw what had been before her eyes all the time. Seizing Nyctasia's outstretched hand, she wrenched off the golden wedding band and flung it from her with all her strength.

Nyctasia cried out like a lost child. At the same time, Shiastred whirled to face Corson, and the full force of his fury struck her before she had time to think. The sky seemed to wheel, and she was crushed to the ground by an agonizing weight. Pain seared her to the bone, but she could not even draw breath to scream. She knew she was dying.

"Kastenid, help me!" Nyctasia called. She stood over Corson, her face like a white-hot flame. Vhar Kastenid walked slowly towards them, his gaze fixed on his enemy, and came to stand at Nyctasia's side.

But Shiastred took no heed of him. Stunned by Nyctasia's betrayal, he stared at her in disbelief and sorrow, but Nyctasia did not waver.

He turned away, then, like a man wounded, walked aimlessly for a few paces, then stopped and pulled off his cloak, holding it out before him. As he tore it across, the air was rent with a shaft of gleaming darkness that blinded the eye.

When sight returned to them, the three who remained found nothing but the sundered cloak where Lord Erystalben had stood. Nyctasia walked slowly over to it and picked it up. "It is always carelessness that defeats one," she said softly.

Vhar Kastenid helped Corson to her feet. "I owe you my life, my friend. I'll not forget your courage. But how did you know?"

"She doesn't wear gold," Corson said brusquely. To her amazement she found herself uninjured. Only minutes before, she had thought that her bones must be crushed to dust. But she felt weak and shaken still. "Let me alone. Look to Her Ladyship."

"I'm sorry," he said gently.

Nyctasia was kneeling on the hard ground, holding the riven cloak tightly against her, her head bowed, her slender frame racked with sobs.

Vhar Kastenid touched her shoulder. "Come home, Lady Nyctasia."

"I have no home!" The tears denied by years of discipline coursed down her face unchecked. "Only now do I know what it is to be an exile. I left everything without regret, but now I have lost myself!"

"What is truly yours cannot be lost or taken," Kastenid said gravely. "Though the heedless may throw it away."

39

WHEN THEY RETURNED, there was no sign of Shiastred's servants—the halls were silent and empty.

"My people will return to me now," said Kastenid, "and I shall be able to show you a more fitting welcome. I would have you treat my home as your own."

Corson was relieved to find the hall deserted. It seemed a different place, and no longer afflicted her with nightmarish memories and forebodings. She took full advantage of Kastenid's hospitality and enjoyed her unaccustomed idleness at first, but soon began to grow restless. Only her concern for Nyctasia made her reluctant to be on her way.

It seemed that nothing would ever rouse Nyctasia from her grief. She barely left her chamber, sitting day after day at the window, long after it grew too dark to see more than the moonlit surface of the quiet pool below. Her will to heal herself had left her.

"Do not war against the *vahn* in this way," Kastenid pleaded with her. "You must allow it to console you. Despair destroys the spirit."

". . . and mourning denies the Discipline," Nyctasia rejoined. She looked up from the piece of sewing that lay across her lap. "I know the Principles as well as you, my friend. But now that I need them the most, I find them hollow. . . . No, the fault is in myself, not in the Discipline, I know that. I am too weak to achieve Balance."

"Then let me help you."

"You've tried to help me before, and you did not find me grateful."

"You know now that I am not your enemy."

"No, I have been my own enemy all the while. You think me as true a *vahnite* as yourself, but I tell you I've done things that would turn you against me if you but knew—"

"You have left Rhostshyl, yet you still dwell within its walls, Edonaris. That life is behind you now."

"Erystalben is part of that life."

He watched her draw the silver needle deftly through the dark cloth. "You follow a dangerous course, my lady."

"What 'Ben did was more dangerous! He couldn't know what awaited him beyond that Threshold. It was madness!"

"It was his only hope of escape."

Nyctasia's voice trembled. "No, he wasn't afraid. He risked that spell rather than strike at me—though I had turned on him!"

"You cannot blame yourself for that, you had no choice. Shiastred used you."

Nyctasia shook her head. "I warned you that I would stand with him—you refused to take me at my word." Her voice grew hard. "I turned to you because I had to protect Corson. But he believed that I'd betrayed him, that is why I must do this, danger or no. He may be dead—I have to know." She shook out the folds of the mended cloak, neatly stitched where Erystalben ar'n Shiastred had torn it.

"I don't believe it either," Corson said. Kastenid had found her in the stable, busy grooming her horse. "But I don't believe much of what Nyc says about anything." She had finished with the curry comb and was going over the animal a second time with a soft brush. Kastenid took up another and began working on the horse's other side.

"She believes it, and as long as she does she'll never be free of him," he said.

"That one's such a clever liar she's begun to believe her own lies."

They worked in silence for a few minutes. Corson knelt and gently ran her fingers down the horse's foreleg. Then, lifting the hoof, she began to clean out the mud and pebbles with a pick.

"I'm afraid of what she may do," he said at last.

Corson looked up at him. "You're in love with her yourself."

He did not deny it. "She will take nothing from me," he said helplessly. "I have won, and yet I am defeated."

40

FOR THE MOST powerful spells, the preparations are the simplest. Nyctasia lifted the heavy mirror from the wall and laid it on the round table, then covered it with Shiastred's cloak. For a long time she only stood there, calm and still, her hands resting on the draped mirror. At last, she silently recited the necessary words, and swept aside the mended cloak.

> Behold in this enchanted mirror
> images reversed but clearer.
> The silent echo of the spirit
> speaks to those who choose to hear it.

Her reflection appeared dim and distant as though seen at the bottom of a dark well. But it was not her own face that she sought in the mirror.

Erystalben knelt at the edge of a pool like black glass, and Nyctasia saw her reflection appear to him in the quiet water. "Why did you do it?" she whispered, and saw that his lips formed the same words. Her tears spilled onto the mirror's surface, making the images waver like broken water. She saw her pale reflection ripple as Shiastred leaned over to touch the pool, and a feeling of faintness came over her. She reached to steady herself against the table but tears blinded her, and her hands closed on empty air. As she fell, her forehead struck sharply against the heavy silver frame of the mirror.

Nyctasia drifted in darkness till a dim light glimmered somewhere above her, and she reached toward it, curious. A hand parted the darkness and clasped hers, drawing her up-ward easily. She stepped from the dark water, her hand still clasped in Erystalben's.

"Forgive me," both said, but no sound broke the unchang-ing stillness. Silent as shadows, then, they came together, and their wordless lips met to say all that was needful between them.

41

CORSON PACED RESTLESSLY about the chamber where Nyctasia had lain all that day, motionless, never waking, hardly seeming to draw breath. To Corson she looked paler and more fragile than ever.

The mirror, cracked and blood-stained, gave back to her a crazed reflection of herself each time she passed by. She found herself trying to avoid the sight of it. Shiastred's cloak still lay at the foot of the table and she kicked it aside, then, puzzled, picked it up. The material was all of a piece—there was not a seam or stitch to show that it had ever been torn. With a shudder, she dropped it over the broken mirror.

Nyctasia opened her eyes and sat up, looking around her in bewilderment. She smiled when she saw Corson. "You're still here, then, my Corson? I'd have thought you'd be on your way to the coast by now."

Corson crossed over to her. "It was only this morning you knocked yourself senseless."

"So it was . . . it seems a long time ago."

"But I would be on my way if you could stay out of trouble for half a day."

"You needn't worry about me," Nyctasia said, taking Corson's hand. "I'm all right now. There's nothing to keep you here."

Corson hesitated. "Well, and what's to keep you here? Why don't you come with me?"

"You know I dare not show my face near Rhostshyl."

"But I've a long way to go before I even reach Mehomne

—I don't mean to cross that rutting forest again! And yᴏ ought to see something of the world before you wall yoursel up in some wizard's den. Besides, you could profit from lessons in swordfighting," Corson reminded her.

Nyctasia toyed absently with one silver earring. "There's something in what you say," she mused.

"We could go south to the Edonaris vineyards and visit your relatives on the way, if you like." She saw a flicker of interest light Nyctasia's wan features.

"That is tempting," she admitted.

"Well, we shouldn't lose any time—I want to reach Lhestreq before the turn of the season. Ships are scarce once the rough weather sets in."

"Will tomorrow suit you?"

"We can't get away from here too soon to suit me. But are you fit to travel?"

Nyctasia lay back against the pillows. "I will be."

Corson bowed low. "With your permission, then, my lady, I shall leave you to your repose."

"Corson . . . I had reason to act the lady with you as I did. The Influences at work here could have destroyed you. Don't you see, I had to drive you away for your own sake, and what better way to do it than to offend your pride? And it worked, but then you came back. . . . I warned you not to interfere . . . when you attacked me, 'Ben knew you for Kasfenid's pawn. He had to deal with you quickly, before Kastenid could recover."

Corson was unconvinced, but she knew it was useless to argue with Nyctasia. "What does it matter now? He's dead, Nyc, forget him."

Nyctasia hesitated. "Well . . . he's *gone.*"

"But isn't he dead?" cried Corson, not concealing her dismay.

Nyctasia looked up at her with a ghost of her old mischievous manner. "I can explain—" she offered.

"Not if I know it!" Corson protested, and hurried from the chamber.

* * *

"I cannot stay here." Nyctasia finished looking through the books she'd brought from Rhostshyl. She chose only one, and

..t it back in her satchel. "I'm no longer as sure as I was . . .
what sacrifices I'm willing to make. I must decide that alone,
Kastenid—away from the Yth and its temptations."

And how to find 'Ben unless she took up her travels again?
But she kept her own counsel as to that.

"Don't you see that together we could hold this place without making the compromises Shiastred was driven to?" he
urged.

"If I'd been with him he'd not have been forced to pay that
price! But the city was in chaos—I hoped I could prevent a
civil war if I stayed. But I only made more enemies for myself, and I failed 'Ben when I knew that he needed me here.
You're well rid of me, I tell you—I'm poison to those who
trust me!"

"You do not know yourself, Nyctasia, but I have tested
you, and I know your true worth. There's no need for you to
run away again—you're making a mistake."

"I've made many," Nyctasia said bitterly. "I'm sorry." She
turned away from him abruptly. "Will you keep these books
for me? I daresay you can make use of them."

"Done."

Nyctasia wrapped Shiastred's long cloak about her, then
took up the black harp and hung it at her back. "I may need
this," she said lightly. "Perhaps I'll have to make my way as a
minstrel."

"Nyc!" Corson shouted from below, "I'm waiting for you!
I told you I want to get an early start."

"Yes, I'm coming," Nyctasia called to her. "I'm ready
now."

42

THE FARTHER THEY traveled from Hlasven, the higher Corson's spirits rose. The cool weather was beginning and the morning was bright and clear. Even Nyctasia grew less subdued and moody as they rode through the ripe, sunlit countryside.

"That fortuneteller wasn't far from the mark after all," Corson remarked. "I've made a dangerous journey, and I'm much the richer for it, but what of the titles and honors he promised me? Why don't you make me a Lady for saving your useless life, you ungrateful whelp?"

"Only the majority of the Rhaicimate can confer a title— and at present I am unfortunately a weak minority. But if ever I regain my authority in Rhostshyl, you'll get all that you deserve, never fear. I'll have you flogged from one end of the city to the other to teach you your place!"

Corson shouted with laughter. This was more the Nyctasia she was used to. "I know what place fate intended for me. The fortuneteller said I'd become a lady of title and influence at the end of the journey."

"Then perhaps the journey isn't over yet," said Nyctasia. "Where are we bound now, oh Lady Corson, favorite of fortune?"

"Time enough you took heed of that! Do you know of the harvest fair at Osela?"

"No. Is it an important market?"

"Asye, what a mooncalf!" Corson said with exasperation. "Don't you know anything but spells and schemes? The Osela fair is famous—there's nothing to match it on the coast. It lasts for weeks, and we'll be there in good time to see everything—dancers, acrobats, troupes of players and mummers, jugglers and conjurors. And there are games and contests, races, wrestling, archery matches. . . ."

"And minstrels, I suppose?" Nyctasia unstrapped her harp and opened the sound-box at the back. She took out the silver key and began turning the pegs to tune the strings.

"Oh yes, singers and harpers and beggars and pickpockets —all the usual rabble."

Nyctasia gave her a dark look. "If I never make a lady of you, Corson, you may yet succeed in making me forget that I am one."

"So much the better for you. What good is a title to you now?"

"What good has it ever been to me, for that matter?" said Nyctasia. She sighed and plucked a chord on the ebonwood harp.

> "Oh, I could complain
> that my life is a curse.
> The grief and the pain
> would fill many a verse.
> But it's best to refrain—
> Things could always be worse!"